Low Tide in the Desert

■ ■ ■

Low Tide
in the Desert

■ ■ ■

Nevada Stories

for Sherry :
an inspired shaper of the arts
and friend .. with appreciation for
her caring about these words.

DAVID KRANES

David

11·23·96
Miami

University of Nevada Press

Reno   Las Vegas

Western Literature Series

A list of books in the series appears at the end of this volume.

University of Nevada Press, Reno, Nevada 89557 USA
Copyright © 1973, 1977, 1978, 1979, 1981, 1985, 1993, 1995,
1996 by David Kranes

Library of Congress Cataloging-in-Publication Data
Kranes, David.
Low tide in the desert : Nevada stories / David Kranes.
p.   cm.   —   (Western literature series)
Contents: Nevada dreams—The Black Friar of Fremont Street—
Slot Queen—The Phantom Mercury of Nevada—The last Las Vegas story—Dealer—
Life on the Moon—Who I am is—Eagle—The whorehouse picnic—Salvage.
ISBN 0-87417-287-X   (pbk. : alk. paper)
I. Title.
PS3561.R26L6   1996   96-22466
813'.54—dc20
CIP

The paper used in this book meets the requirements of American
National Standard for Information Sciences—Permanence of Paper
for Printed Library Materials, ANSI Z39.48-1984.
Binding materials were selected for strength and durability.

The author gratefully acknowledges the original publishers of these stories: "Dealer,"
Esquire (August 1973); "Slot Queen," *Ascent* (1977); "The Black Friar of Fremont
Street," *Confrontation* (1978); "Who I Am Is," *New Lazarus Review* (1978); "Life on
the Moon," *New Lazarus Review* (1978); "The Phantom Mercury of Nevada," *Hunters
in the Snow* (1979); "Eagle," *Tales from the Southwest* (1981); "The Whorehouse
Picnic," *Writer's Forum* (Fall 1985); "Nevada Dreams," *Story* (1993); "The Last Las
Vegas Story," *Gulf Stream Magazine* (1995).

First Printing

05   04   03   02   01   00   99   98   97   96   5   4   3   2   1

For Jeff Metcalf
who has been in the same desert
and in the same tide

Contents

Nevada Dreams

Nevada wakes up before her alarm in her half-trailer, which sits atilt on a rock shelf in the Spanish Springs Valley at the foot of the Virginia Mountains, and she smells the Basco's blood. It's not the Basco him*self,* of course—*his* blood—it's the lamb he slaughtered for Easter last night. The Basco lives in the trailer's other half—there with his wools and vegetable dyes and loom—and hates being called the Basco; he says his name is Emmett Laxalt. But people don't always get called what they want—Nevada knows; still, it can be good, because it keeps pride from running in herds like the horses Wild Horse Annie has wanted to save. So it's either good or bad: to not call someone by their name; Nevada chooses good. The Basco is a fine weaver though and a fine man, fine enough not to worry about what he's called, but Nevada wishes the smell of the blood hadn't found its way through their common wall, especially with the snow falling. She's probably breathed the blood all night without knowledge and will probably carry it to her job, making change at the Comstock. Still, the Basco has been good in his pledge to cook them Easter dinner. He's outside, even now, moving the stones to line his fire pit. A flame leaps up: he has set a match to the cedar tinder; it's his way of saying good morning. The cedar tinder will inflame the logs that will make the coals to roast the lamb. They are not lovers, though both know the Basco has certainly had that in his head. They only share halves of this twin trailer out of need, out of circumstance. So he is good, the Basco—Nevada having said *no* and then *no* again, twice, during the last year—to nevertheless care for her and try to make this Easter Day proper. Because there are other men and other places Nevada dreams of and hopes for. There are other lives she imagines.

Nevada was not born but came here: to this place—this Reno, this valley, these hills, this nearly bottomless lake. And her name has been only briefly Nevada. Before, it was two names—Iona and Gallegos, Iona Gallegos, the first before the second and both from the country of Guatemala. On her way moving north in bursts and angles—hiding, working, taking flight—her English poor, when people asked, "What's-yourname?" she thought herself asked, "Where'reyougoing?" and answered (because she'd heard of jobs there with no green cards) "Nevada." So, sixteen-seventeen-eighteen, then—working fields, cleaning a thousand overnight rooms—that became her name: she simply stopped being Iona Gallegos, daughter of the singing Elena Gallegos, and started being Nevada.

She has been Nevada now for nearly a dozen years and in this trailer for six. Still she remembers herself before. She remembers Iona Gallegos—the child, the emerging woman and daughter of her singing mother—and remembers their small home outside Puerto Barrios. She remembers being daughter of her father too, though he was nearby so seldom, appearing only with other men sometimes, all with guns, and there would be a meal—pig, lamb somehow suddenly instead of roots, beans, fried bread. And they would all eat, the men, like filthy ghosts, growling but laughing and making jokes with Elena Gallegos, her singing mother. But then they would all be gone in the morning. And Nevada remembers the Caribbean too, where she and her mother occasionally swam, there in the Gulf of Honduras. And she remembers sounds of planes. And of guns. And of men's voices traveling to them over speakers—like but *not* like the Comstock's "Mechanic to slot 273, please! Mechanic to slot 273!"—more, really, like dark birds with huge wings trying to fly, the wings ripping in the air; sounds, tearing and terrible and impossible to sing away.

And finally, what Nevada remembers about where she lived first near Puerto Barrios was the men who came and began asking her singing mother, Elena, questions. About her father. How they seemed nice and made jokes (one gave her a paper bird). But when her mother refused to answer and only sang—louder and louder—the men grew angry and struck her; then Nevada remembers how sure she'd been something terrible would happen. And how it had. Or hadn't. It's so hard now to know. Nevada remembers night. She remembers the men pulling her mother, still singing, outside and starting the engine of their truck and stringing small wires with clamps from under the hood (Nevada obscured in the bordering trees), how they revved the truck—Elena Gallegos, her mother, singing all the more: proudly and sweetly over the growling truck— and how the men set their clamps to her mother's tongue. And Nevada remembers what seemed then to be a miracle: the sound of her mother's voice, her mother's tongue, like a bulb, lit in her mouth. And then it all going black. The night. The scene. Her mother's mouth and then whole face, black like burnt neon. And then one of the men saying, "*Está muerta*," another disconnecting the wires and the clamps, the three climbing back into the truck and driving away.

Finally, too, Nevada remembers remembering her mother's words: "*Corre. Corre hacia el norte. Si algo pasa . . . corre hacia el norte.*" (Run. Run north. If anything happens . . . run north), and so, fifteen only that night but *doing* that: running. North. *What'syourname? / Where'reyougoing? . . . Nevada.*

And so, yes; in one way, it's a terrible place Nevada's come from and that visits her still sometimes, slipping behind her eyes, refusing disregard. And perhaps her life, making change, riding her trail bike to and from, being a woman nearly alone except for the Basco in these weed-and-stone-colored hills— perhaps all of this might appear to be without grace and to hold no future. But Nevada dreams! Of course, partly it is herself; but partly it is this land she's come to, filled, from first conquests, with its immense *permission*. Dreams! And she has seen huge birds, blue birds, work their wings over the green bays of Pyramid Lake and a Vietnamese woman win more than a million dollars on a MegaBucks. And every day, almost, she dreams her mother's tongue—all song, all light. So—dreaming, seeing—Nevada knows, for instance, that in America there are cowboys who speak the poetry of their some- times-in-the-icy-wind working lives into microphones. She has heard them! In this very state! They're *real*. And even the Basco tells stories, and she has seen *him*, his shirt like a silk flower on the ground, lift a cut ponderosa log over his head nearly a hundred times. So: if one good-then-better thing becomes possible, Nevada believes yet-the-next-better thing might also, and so she practices what she practices: *gratitude, patience,* and *hope*. She has told the Basco that much. It's become a joke, but a true one, between them. When she refused the last time to come with the Basco to his bed, he fixed his jaw briefly. There were hooks in his eyes that scared Nevada. He pressed his lips with a sadness even Nevada could see—but then he said, "Well . . . gratitude, patience, hope . . . no problem. I've got time."

When Nevada hauls her trail bike from her half-trailer to set off for the Comstock, the Basco says, "Good morning, my dear" and sweeps a hat down through the nearly-five-o'clock dark, parting the ash-dry snow and scattering it.

"Good morning," Nevada says and walks her bike over to what's become a full fire in the pit.

"Beautiful scarf!" the Basco says. It was a gift, one he wove for her. Wove especially.

Nevada smiles. She sees the lamb, covered by a small tarpaulin, and can taste, suddenly on the roof of her mouth and behind her nose, its now-oiled spices and blood. "Nice fire," she says. She sees the Basco grinding leaves in a stoneware bowl. "What are those?" she asks.

"Herbs," he says. "More herbs."

She asks, "What herbs?"

He tells her, "Secret."

"Of course," Nevada says and smiles.

"You know what?" the Basco says—proud, suddenly grinning.

"What?" Nevada says.

"Someone . . . going to give you a big tip today," he says.

"Good," Nevada says. "Good; I need it. I need all the tips I can get." And she starts her bike. "Just us two?" she asks. ". . . All that lamb?" She calls her questions over the bike's drone.

The Basco shrugs.

"So . . . maybe I'll invite my—I don't know—boyfriend," Nevada says, then realizes she's pushed her playfulness too far. "Just kidding," she says.

"Of course," the Basco says and rocks back on his heels from the flame of his fire.

Then Nevada begins—along the packed trail that will take her, two miles, to Nevada 445. The Basco's wine and gold and here-and-there-turquoise scarf beats the wind behind her.

Reno's lights announce themselves halfway, and she's at the rear of the Comstock a good ten minutes before morning shift, which starts at six. She locks her bike, goes in, hangs her down vest and scarf in her locker, retrieves her jacket, and is on the floor fully three minutes before the hour. The slots are busy for a Sunday morning. But it's Easter. By seven, an off-duty fry cook from Fitzgerald's hits a quarter progressive for over four thousand and gives Nevada a hundred: "You gave me the dollars that I used!" he says. She smiles. The Basco's already a prophet; it seems a good day.

At nine-thirty, she breaks for breakfast and sits eating hot seven-grain cereal in the coffee shop with her friend the dealer Arnelle, who tells Nevada she did too much cocaine the night before. "*Any* much is too much," Nevada says.

"Any much is too much!" Arnelle repeats. She coughs a laugh. "That's good! I have to remember that." Then Arnelle tells Nevada her father's threatened to come in from Albu-querque. "I'm on pins and needles," Arnelle says.

Often Nevada can only guess at things that Arnelle says— what they mean. But she likes her friend; she likes her laugh; it sounds like the beach waves pulling back on the Gulf of Honduras. She likes her fleshiness as well and her frosted hair. Arnelle has helped Nevada write her application to move from making change to dealing. Sometimes, when they break, Arnelle gives lessons with a single deck, assuring Nevada she's a natural; it's just time. What Nevada likes most about Arnelle is that she's encouraging.

Back on the floor, Nevada gets another twenty dollars; it's a woman whose "Jokers Wild" has just unloaded two hundred coins. And then, circulating, Nevada sees a man with a yellow mustache taking his turn at the dice table. And Nevada knows the man because she's seen him—eyes like trout-holding water behind a rock—seen him in Elko standing in front of a microphone. The man's a cowboy from near Dixie Valley. And poet. And Poet. She remembers him saying:

I know what fills my heart
and know what hurts.
I sew the buttons on
my own work shirts.

And remembers, as well, him singing about his sheepdog, a dog, Nevada recalls, named Tall, who—the Cowboy Poet sang—could filet bones from German Browns caught in the Humboldt Salt Marsh outlets.

Nevada moves nearly beside the Cowboy, the Poet, who has just made an eight and had the table cheer and feels, partly, that it's her admiration that has brought him luck, her wishing him all that she can wish, having loved his voice and words so much in Elko.

His name is Wayne McCloud; she remembers and says, without planning, "Wayne McCloud," and with her saying, Wayne McCloud turns and studies her and grins, his yellow mustache taking a turn, as on an axle, just above his lip; his body gently pressing a Stetson between himself and the dice table, leaning soft against it, Nevada thinks, as though it were a woman. Her words, his name, still trail lightly in the air. Like the smell of bacon. Like cigarette smoke. *Wayne McCloud.*

"In the flesh!" he says. "In the flesh . . . and winning!" He laughs.

Nevada remembers his laugh; he laughed over the microphone in Elko when he didn't mean to, then said, "Oops," and it tripped chills between her shoulders.

"You stay there!" Wayne McCloud instructs, and he turns back, lifts the dice and rolls an eleven. The table cheers. Wayne McCloud raises his fist over his head. He shouts, "Let it ride!"

Eight other players shout back, "Let it ride!" and with their shout, Wayne McCloud circles an arm out and into the air, which he clearly expects Nevada to step into, under, so he can pull her close.

She does. He does. He rolls a seven and the entire table applauds. He sings a line—no guitar—"Some days it's all where you are," and Nevada remembers the line, remembers the song. She's so nervous she can barely breathe. Wayne McCloud squeezes her; he calls her Peach.

For the next fifteen minutes, Wayne McCloud wins money and more money. Nevada says she should be on the floor, but Wayne says, "Not a chance," and DeGrazzi, the pit boss, nods to her, "No problem; you're fine," so Nevada relaxes. And when Wayne McCloud finishes winning, and after he's given her two black chips, Nevada reveals her seeing him in Elko. She says, "You said this . . . you sang that," and she remembers verses and Wayne McCloud lights up and says, "Well, I'll be a gelding's dick!" Then apologizes. So then Nevada invites him, after work, up to Spring Valley for an Easter dinner.

Wayne McCloud smiles. "You've got it!" he says, then, "Say, you're a pretty woman. You married?"

And Nevada blushes and says no. Then, because she feels she must, she tells Wayne McCloud that it won't be just them; they won't be alone. Her friend the Basco will be there.

"Who?" Wayne McCloud asks.

"Emmett," Nevada says. "My friend Emmett. He's the one who's cooking the lamb."

"Sounds like a winner," Wayne McCloud says—though he seems unsure.

"How's Tall?" Nevada asks, remembering Wayne's wonderful Brown Trout poem. "How's your dog, Tall?" It makes her glad to ask the question.

But Wayne McCloud only shivers—blown somehow by a blast of snow. The trout behind the rock pools in his eyes move laterally. He doesn't answer at first, and Nevada knows memory pictures are in his head: she has them in hers. *It's okay,* she wants to say; *it doesn't matter,* but Wayne cuts in. "He's mostly stupid these days," he says. "He got kicked in the head."

"By a cow?" Nevada manages.

"No—stupid sheepherder," Wayne McCloud says.

And his words seem to set them both thinking . . . but then they agree on a time—two-thirty—to meet back at the very table and move separate ways.

So now Nevada has three hundred and twenty dollars and works on with the knowledge that she will be having Easter dinner with the Cowboy Poet, Wayne McCloud. *America . . .* then *Nevada,* she thinks. Men with trout behind their eyes say poems into microphones . . . and you can meet them . . . and share bread. She has paid attention; she has seen and heard; she has dreamed and there is proof—*again,* she feels, *again*—that dreams come true.

So she works the floor: gives change—gives quarters, dimes, gives nickels. She fills in for her friend Anita on the Aurora Carousel, handing out trays of dollars. A blond girl in a rabbit-skin coat and leather skirt wins two thousand for three blue sevens and gives Nevada another hundred. Nevada has never had this kind of day. When Anita gets back, Nevada tries giving the hundred to her, but Anita says, "No, split," so they do. And when it's done, Nevada takes her own five minutes to walk outside because she's sure it will have stopped snowing and that the streets will be warm. And she's right: the sun's nearly overhead like ripe fruit, and the day, in fact, has that taste: ginger-root, plantain, lemon rind.

When she meets Wayne McCloud, he is very drunk, so drunk it frightens her. His words don't light up like her mother's tongue anymore but spill like sludge oil. She wonders if she should say no, even lie: say the lamb caught fire and burned up . . . is only bone, bone only. But Wayne McCloud—standing there in his soft leather coat, his guitar in a canvas jacket slung over his shoulder—seems incredibly sad; he seems a sad poet and there should be sad poets too, or sad poet *days*: not every poem, not every song, needs to make you wish and hope and smile.

So Nevada says nothing. But how should they get back? That's a question. Wayne McCloud has a Ford pickup, but he's drunk and knows—"I couldn't drive a calf with the dry heaves!" he says. And then he asks her—as though she might have the answer—"Why am I drunk? Why did I do this?"

"I can't tell" is all Nevada can say.

"Is it a secret?" Wayne McCloud asks. He's serious.

Nevada shrugs.

"I hate myself when I do this," Wayne McCloud confesses. "It's a stupid choice. It's a very stupid choice. This is not me. This is rarely me. This is some kind of dumb version of . . . something," Wayne McCloud says. And then he asks: "Do you know what I'm saying?"

"I might," Nevada says.

"I'm very angry at myself," Wayne McCloud says.

Nevada nods.

"I *did* keep my money, though. *That's* good."

How will they get there? Wayne McCloud has his pickup, but Nevada has no license. Applying, she's been told, might get her deported. So Wayne McCloud climbs onto the back of Nevada's unlicensed trail bike, and when he does the wheels seem only half as far from the ground. Still, the bike moves; the bike goes forward—Wayne McCloud laughing now like three birds all in the air at the same time, his guitar thumping like an oil drum—and they move along.

It's not the *best* ride. Wayne falls off four times—once rolling almost under the tires of a semi heading south toward Sparks and making Nevada scream—then slyly rolling away just in time and scrambling to his feet. "Had you going there—didn't I?!" Nevada's heart pumps and hammers. She feels angry. She nods yes and says, "Don't" and then, "Don't do that . . . or you can't come," and he apologizes. In fact, Wayne McCloud cries, "Why? Why did I do this?!" And when he cries, he shakes so that he can't stay on the back of Nevada's bike and they have to wait, on the shoulder of Nevada 445, until his crying's done with.

But they manage and make it finally. On the approach, Nevada sees her dear, patient friend, the Basco, at the crest of the hill just above the trailer, and she knows he's been on the lookout and worried. Nevada waves. The Basco's mittened hand, bone-colored in the air, speaks to her, its own language, and the word spoken is "uncertainty." He's a good man. Nevada's late. He has seen another person behind her on the bike. She wonders now whether she has made a choice that might not be the right one.

Still, when Nevada and Wayne McCloud pull up, the Basco has run down on his snowshoes and is waiting with a broad smile. Nevada makes introductions. She calls the Basco "my friend Emmett," and she can tell the Basco likes that. The Cowboy Poet and the Basco shake hands. "Smells damn fine!" Wayne McCloud says. "Somethin' here!" He produces a bottle of Jack Daniel's Black from one pocket of his long, soft leather coat and a bottle of Irish Mist from the other: "We don't have to drink these," he says, "but they're my contribution. In fact, don't let me have any—I've had enough!"

It's well past four; the valley is almost all shadows, no visible sun—except a small flame at the top of bare ridgetop trees. The Basco has a separate fire blazing for warmth. He's set one of his own woven pieces—black, gold, silver—over the outside table. There's a large cut-glass vase with piñon and yew boughs arranged—cones and berries. "You'd make any woman ashamed of being a woman," Nevada tells him.

She hopes her words to be especially nice, but they freeze in the air, somehow, like a bad announcement, and no one seems to know what to do with them.

"Are you ashamed of being a woman . . . living here with me?" the Basco asks. It's sincere but freezes midair the same way.

Wayne McCloud moves over near the Basco's loom and unzips the case of his guitar, starts tuning. The Basco undoes the screwcap on Wayne McCloud's gift of whiskey. He pours some into glasses, hands the glasses around. "To Our Lord," he proposes. Wayne McCloud regards his glass, uncertain. He studies the Basco, runs his tongue over his lips. They all drink, repeating, "To Our Lord" / "To Our Lord." It is a Thanksgiving and an Easter and a moment outside of time. Framed, the three look like three figures in a painting.

Nevada asks, before they eat, if Wayne might say a poem and he does. It seems, momentarily, to sober him. He says one about an old rancher with just a single eye whose best friend is his three-legged dog; the poem's called "Stumbling toward Love." Wayne McCloud's own voice cracks and nearly breaks. It makes Nevada cry and, during it, she looks over and sees the Basco running his hand, back and forth, over the shuttle of his loom.

They take their seats. The Basco has placed Nevada beside himself, himself across from Wayne McCloud. The valley is dark now; the foothills barely marked against the night. There's a glow, though, from the fire pit, almost as if it comes from a deep underground—from another, a further, world. The Basco attempts a joke: he says one day the whole state will be lit from beneath—like what they see. Dig a hole; the earth will shine its own haunting lights into the sky. He says all the lakes will be like green neon bulbs. His words twist Nevada's memory to a chill. There's an uncertain laughter, the Basco laughing more than the other two.

"He means the testing," Nevada explains, but her mind

moves back and forth like a white-tailed deer in a clearing.

"And the dump sites," the Basco says. "They going to make a new volcano out of Yucca Mountain."

No one laughs this time. Wayne McCloud can't keep himself from staring, it seems, at the Basco. Caught doing it, he takes his hat off, takes his hair in a fist for only a moment, resets his hat, and fills everybody's whiskey glass.

Nevada wants both men to like each other. She smiles first at one, then the other. She thinks to turn the conversation to sheep because they are in the hills here and it is a subject the Basco knows. She remembers, only after she's introduced it, that Wayne McCloud's dog, Tall, has been kicked by a sheepherder in the head. Wayne McCloud drains his glass and recites an off-color poem titled "Muttonshit." "Which is not to say," he tries, drunk again and ungainly in his recovery, "which is not to say, of course . . . that this is not an absolutely delicious dinner. Dead sheep . . . cooked . . . are wonderful. What's the green vegetable?"

The Basco says it's a kind of marsh grass.

"Marsh gas?" the Cowboy Poet tries. He apologizes for his bad joke. "That's a stupid pun," he says. "Stupid . . . stupid pun. Don't let me drink any more."

The Basco empties then fills his own whiskey glass. Wayne McCloud watches him. Nevada tries turning the conversation to trout. She thinks maybe it will prompt Wayne McCloud to think of Tall before his head-kicking and remember when he was so clever, and she knows how the Basco loves fish. Fishing.

The two men end up shouting at one another: The Basco only fishes with lures and flies; he calls the Poet a "meathead" and a "butcher" for using salmon eggs.

"I *eat* all the fish I catch," Wayne McCloud says, then gestures toward their meal. "Who's the butcher?" he says.

"Please," Nevada says.

"You're a Basque . . . *are*n't you!" Wayne McCloud says.

"You're one of . . . !"

"He's an *American*," Nevada says.

"I'm a *Basque!*" The Basco says. "Basque! Basque! Basco!" He leaps up from the table, breaks into song, moves his feet; by his own firelight, they are being treated to a traditional dance.

Wayne McCloud observes. There's admiration: not a doubt—it's in his eyes; Nevada can see—but then a craziness sweeps in and he shouts: "If sheep didn't spend all their stupid time pissing in the water, there'd be enough trout for everybody *and they'd grow bigger.*"

Nevada asks both men, please . . . *please,* don't argue, then asks if either has been to the Mustang Ranch. She hates her question. She hates thinking of women like herself doing what they do there in those trailers (she's seen; she's driven past), those rooms. Still, this *is* its own state, and Nevada guesses that—both men being single—it might be a common ground. So she asks. And both men stop. And look at her. And then they look at each other. There's a silence.

". . . He doesn't need to—he's got his sheep," Wayne McCloud finally offers. His words move around, grumbling, in his mustache.

"And you've got your three-legged dog," the Basco returns.

Wayne McCloud's eyes flare.

"I wish we could all laugh!" Nevada says. But there's a new silence . . . which gets worse—so bad the tamarack branches snapping in the fire pit sound like ground strafing. Finally the Basco barks a laugh, mock, which opens up, like a hole, in silence again . . . and then the silence opens into the Basco's question, straight across the table: "Wayne . . . ?"

Nevada knows—hearing one word, the name, Wayne . . . ?— knows *trouble.*

"Wayne? I just cur'ous," the Basco says, ". . . how you getting *back* tonight?"

"He can stay," Nevada says quickly.

"Where?" the Basco asks.

"Here," Nevada says.

"No," the Basco says.

"You have some room," Nevada says.

"No, I don't," the Basco says.

"Well, then . . . "

"No," the Basco says.

"No *what*?" Nevada finds herself getting angry; the Basco is not being who he can be.

"No, he's *not* staying with *you*," the Basco says.

"Well . . . " Nevada feels her words sputtering like bacon fat. "Well, that's not yours to say," she manages.

"Well . . . I won't *let* him."

"Hey . . . " Wayne McCloud holds his hands out; the wind, a partner to his dance. "Hey . . . if the lady wants me in her bed for the night . . . "

"No! That's not what I said," Nevada says.

"Funny: it sounded to me like . . . "

"You can use my couch," Nevada says.

"No. He *can't*. No, he *can't* use your couch," the Basco says. "He uses your couch . . . I come in . . . I throw him out."

The Cowboy grabs the Jack Daniel's and skips the glass. The neck of the bottle pops out of his mouth on the hit like a cork. Whiskey sprays up his nose. *"Throw me out! Throw me out!"* he mocks. "You couldn't throw *shit* with a *chainsaw!*"

"Gentlemens . . . gentlemens . . . !" Nevada tries.

"Couldn't throw . . . No, but *you* could—I *heard* you!" the Basco says. He coughs. The night air, sweeping off the snow and rocks, has an edge like chewed iron, and it's hit and circled his throat.

Suddenly both men are up and moving and away from the table. The Basco's got a big and curved shearing knife in his glove, which keeps winking in the firelight. Wayne McCloud's fist is around the neck of the Irish Mist bottle. "You're a dead man!" he tells the Basco.

Nevada imagines the word "stop." It's in her brain, nearly in her mouth, but at first it's so small it's not even a ground squirrel a mile away. And the men—the Basco leading now—flare on.

"Then my ghost . . . gonna feed you balls to my sheep . . . all fried up like *scones!*" the Basco says.

Wayne McCloud hooks a wide arc with his bottle.

"*Stop!*" Nevada finally gets the word out—announces it, proclaims it nearly, and both men do: they *stop*. Then she says again—tears now, urgency—looking first to her friend the Basco, then to the Cowboy Poet, Wayne McCloud: "Stop. Stop this. This is Easter." And Nevada cries. Outright. Yet speaks on to be heard through her anguish. "Stop this. This is Easter. Our Lord *died*. Our Lord gave up his life. But lives. Lives, and we blessed Him, blessed His name. Before we shared our Easter dinner. 'To Our Lord.' I never told you, Basco, but my mother . . . " Nevada can't go on, can't utter, she is crying so hard. But both men wait because they see her need and feel her power and she recovers. "My mother . . . my mother died singing a song," Nevada says. "Her tongue lit up in her mouth . . . like the moon. And I saw her. And I see her. Every day, every night . . . in the sky of my life. My mother gave up her life for me . . . so that I might live. . . . This is America. We are American people. We are all from—yes—different places. But this is our land. And this is our food." She gestures—to the nearby, to the close—where they have all been together. "Look! Look: our table. Our food. Are we strangers . . . ? Have we not shared this lamb? . . . this delicious lemon rice . . . this bread—these things? No one will be without a bed. No one will be without a bed tonight. No one will be without a friend."

And like other moments before—Nevada's words knit up a picture in the air—the patience of them, the gratitude, their hope. And the moment is a stopped moment—like one by the painter Goya or the painter El Greco.

And both men set down what they have picked up ruth-lessly and in anger. The Basco his knife into a sheath on a hanging belt. The Cowboy Poet the Irish Mist bottle, which he immediately uncorks and hands on to Nevada, who pauses at first, then lifts it and drinks, handing it on to the Basco, who drinks in turn and hands the bottle back to Wayne McCloud.

Both men are crying now—silently, ashamed. The Basco wanders to his loom. His fingers play and he moves its shuttle, as though weaving the flinty air, the dim crescent moon. And Wayne McCloud, the Cowboy Poet, moves himself aside and looks up, up and out over the ridges of hills, and he begins speaking a poem: "It's called 'Branding in Winter,'" he says, really to himself; his words are quiet.

And Nevada, between them, begins to sing. Near where the Basco had arranged it that morning and begun the flame and where the earth is still opened in its light, Nevada squares herself against the stars and becomes the child of her mother. From the dull, childish landscape, it rises up. Nevada sings.

The Black Friar
of Fremont Street

Call had grown up with hedges and wallpapered rooms. He
had shoveled snow. He had been a pyromaniac for a month—
then a magician. His father'd taken him on professional medi-
cal rounds, every Sunday at dawn. Call believed in the Dying.
And the Atlantic Ocean had not been very far away. He'd collected butterflies—red admirals, mourning cloaks, swallow-
tails, *everywhere,* pinned on spreading boards, "like spirits,"
he told a friend, fiery, clean in his small room's available light.
And Call had felt a friendship with Christ. His grandmother'd
whispered, "Call—Christ made a present of his flesh!" Call
had swum as much as he could under water. He'd felt weight-
less in it. And he'd hidden in closets. He'd held his breath
and blacked out. Once, wandering the Greatest Show on
Earth, he'd stopped in front of a Human Pincushion.

 After the age of reason, though, things grew tough. Call

knew enough not to be crazy. His family's friends seemed a colony of logicians. He did not want to violate any of their trust. He trained himself. His grades improved. He won a third place in the state class B discus. He was an officer in the Forum Club. He customized his own '47 Pontiac. He lifted weights. He got a tan.

At Amherst, he affiliated with a fraternity. He discovered the Dark Ages and Rembrandt. That was sophomore year. Then he met Penny Peterson. Penny had an enormous sailboat, stocked with half-gallon bottles of gin. Penny with the Light! Senior year opened like a cathedral door. Winter Carnival, Call walked naked out into swirling snow, casting beer nuts to jays—but he was drunk. In April, he nailed Columbia Law School's acceptance to the door and played tennis. Ponds filled with ducks! He felt approval broadcast from every lawn in the Greater Boston Area. He had overcome abandon and awe; he had stayed his dark beginnings. And he was almost ready.

The World prepared him. It gave him measurable congratulation. It allowed him to court Sharon Whitesides by the Boston Aquarium. How she dazzled! Call received praise, at his final moot court, for both his brief and his wool plaid J. August suit. His second child was a boy. Life was increase. His house in Gloucester was over two hundred years old. His parents didn't change a thing in the bedroom of his earliest days. Sharon loved antiques. Call earned enough, on one single case, to buy a sailboat; its spinnaker—powder blue. His high school track coach, meeting him on the street, recalled his name and year. He was asked to be a deacon in his parish. And more! His umbrella never broke. Sharon stayed thin. Sometimes, though, he would daydream about the Black Death, or find himself at lunch hour standing in front of Rembrandt's impenetrable and silent shadows in the Boston Museum. More and more, he walked barefoot. But this was all before he set down, ever, in Las Vegas.

He was flying to Salt Lake City. It was March. He had a case involving copper. Salt Lake International Airport was snowbound. His flight circled for an hour, then went on. It landed at McCarran Airport. Salt Lake would be clear by morning. Call's appointment wasn't until the afternoon. There were palm trees! Call couldn't adjust. And the air was warm! Call's entire flight was put up in the Sun 'N Sand. He had a drink, then walked outside. The night was stunned with near-apocalyptic light. Call wandered down Las Vegas Boulevard until he came to the Frontier Hotel. He went inside. Inside, light was almost the same. *People rose from the dead in light like this!* he thought. But it passed. He walked around. The place boomed with shouts and laughter, and with alarms. Call saw money moving. He saw denominations—$5, $25, $100, $500—on the chips. "This is a fun house for suicides!" he heard some person say.

Call played that night. It was the first official venturing of his life. He knew no rules. He guessed. He followed others. He won a hundred and thirty dollars. He bought a showgirl a drink. His face felt radiant. His chest felt stuffed. He had a fleeting memory of the Human Pincushion. It confused his vision. Blackness hung in visible sacks all throughout the light. Call felt short of breath. "Christ . . ." Call started to say something vaguely theological to the showgirl. "Pardon me?" she said.

Returned, Call couldn't sleep. He wasn't happy until he'd risen from his bed, dressed, found a smaller, closer casino, and lost half of what he'd won. "I won one hundred and thirty dollars!" he told Sharon, back in Gloucester, after his trip. He didn't tell her about the loss.

Call's dreams changed. Black dogs growled in them. Earth gave way. He fell. His hand came off when he was greeting a client. He went blind. His house was being burglarized—by himself. He had no money in any of his bank accounts. His daughter, Lisa, was a runaway in New Mexico. Sharon was sunbathing in a cocoon of mud. He was in a walk-in refrigerator, confused. That dream, the refrigerator dream, repeated. It repeated again. He woke up shivering. But their bedroom in Gloucester was drenched with April sun.

"Call—what's happening?" Sharon asked him.

"I feel very…" He couldn't finish his thought. In his mind he saw his father's patients turning gray in the hospital.

In May, Call flew away to Los Angeles. He had to meet with the board of a components company that was considering a merger. "We're heading up," the chairman told him, "and we need to *do* something about it." Call counseled them. On his way back to Boston, he stopped over in Las Vegas.

This time he stayed downtown. He walked the length of Fremont Street, up and down, moving in and out of casino after casino: light and heat. Call felt ignition going on somewhere inside him, smoldering rags. Someone had soaked them in oil and then tossed them there, years ago. And they were kindling.

"What did I ever do to you?!" a derelict passing him on the street mumbled. Call paused and studied him.

He had some extra money, two hundred dollars. It marked a drumbeat in his billfold. He took a hundred out and lost it, lost it fast. He felt small flames licking around his eyes. He took out a second hundred. His hands were shaking. Once, when he'd been very young, he had gone away to the ocean. He had gotten sunburned: Everywhere—the sun! That night he'd shaken like he was shaking now. He'd been sure of death. Positive! Then God had come. An indestructible domed presence over his bed had explained: "Was Mrs. Giornelli afraid—when your father took you into her room with him last Sunday at the hospital?" "No!" Call had answered. Fevered, he had seen the drab slug that was Mrs. Giornelli in her sheets suddenly *up*, aloft and fiery, as a Queen or Painted Lady or Viceroy, floating in the sun. A febrile thrill had buzzed in him. It buzzed in him now. He touched the checkbook in his other pocket.

It took forty-five minutes to get credit at the Union Plaza. Call made his check out for three hundred more. He lost a hundred immediately. He drank B&Bs. He lost another fifty. Call put *all* of fifty on the pass line. The roller made four immediate passes. Now Call had four hundred out. He threw a B&B down. Logic told him: *Pull it back!* But he left it. The shooter passed again, and Call felt strangely abandoned. Who had left? Rags, somewhere, burst into sooty flame. Call pulled his money back now. He held it in his hands—green discs and wafers. Something his grandmother had said . . .

He walked around again. He went from place to place: street to tables to street. He looked at people, wondered who they were. A word began to follow him, *trail* him like a secret agent. The word was "mendicant." He saw men take out markers for two, three, four, five thousand dollars. He thought, God, I'd like to do that. Call saw them lose their markers. It seemed abstract—like theology—nothing real, no real money; just the slips of paper and the tokens. And the ritual! Tremendous ritual! He wondered what a person had to do to set up so high a credit line.

Call lost over three hundred dollars of the four hundred and fifty he had been ahead. "I won a hundred and seventeen dollars stopping over in Vegas," he told Sharon when he got home.

It grew. Call started being more involved in his church. He read the *Letters of Saint Ignatius*. He took the Eucharist. He read Tillich and Bultmann. He felt that Bultmann, shearing myth from the New Testament, was a thief. He said as much to Sharon.

"I don't understand what you're saying," she said to him.

He exchanged his blue for a gray spinnaker. He remembered playing CYO baseball.

He read Saint Francis's *Canticle of the Sun.* "Above all," it said, "Brother Sun." What was that? It had been composed in a San Damiano garden. Call made another "stopover" in Vegas. He lost nearly two hundred and fifty dollars. He spent the night at the Sands. His room had mirrors on strange, unexpected walls. Call kept startling himself—though the washed, thinner man reflected didn't seem, really, startled at *all.* More than one of him seemed to be staying there, at any rate seemed to come and go. He had another version of his refrigerator dream.

Call didn't mention the losing stopover to Sharon. He bought her a set of brandy snifters, though. He dreamed his son, Carver, suffered a concussion playing football. There was a power shortage at the Gloucester Hospital. Sharon was weeping—terror in the sound, and agony. But he was looking on it with a kind of curiosity. How would God enlist the services of Carver? he was wondering.

He read Loyola's *Exercises.* Loyola had exchanged his military clothes with a beggar. He read Augustine's *City of God.* He tore his hands trimming rosebushes on a Sunday and watched them bleed—slowly, raggedly—with a fascination. He took a thousand dollars from his savings and bent a trip to Minneapolis to make another "stopover."

He lost it all: slowly at first and then rapidly. It moved away from him inevitably as the tide. Call watched it go. He knew it was going. He knew it would continue to go. And yet he set it out. He laid it down and set it out. There was a small ribbon of electricity that tingled around his skull—a message from the Greater Inevitability of his brain, relayed from his brain to his body—which was telling him: *It is all going away.*

Everything that you place there is going. His eyes—he could feel them—were wired to the same message and charge. Still he did it, set his chips in the current—and watched. He felt his clothes dropping from his body. He was being stripped in a public square. There was *that* kind of humiliation. Others at the table were watching. People behind him! Call felt strangely satisfied, strangely clean.

When it was all gone, Call checked every pocket. He found four dollars more. He set them down on roulette. They went. They went away. He took all his change. He fed it into slot machines. He won five dollars but rejected every quarter of it back. Nothing stayed.

Nothing remained: not a bill, not a coin. Call walked out onto Fremont Street. He had nothing! People came and went. They made black, eddying gaps in the light. Call tried moving with them. But it wouldn't work. He walked down a side street, into an alley. Newspaper had blown there in scraps. Call felt the rags inside his body smoking, flaming. He felt crazily warmed. Should he sleep here? Should he rustle the crumpled paper and the broken glass with his fitful sleep? What was happening? Call sensed silence. He had a room with his luggage in it. He had credit cards. What was Sharon doing—at that very moment? She was wonderful! Really! She was so pacific! Would she sense any of his humility?

Call walked back to the street. He watched the people again. He stopped a woman. "Ma'am, I'm sorry. But I just spent every cent I have. I didn't realize what was happening. Do you have ...? I need—well, a room."

The woman studied Call's expensive suit. She took her wallet out. They exchanged addresses. She gave Call a twenty.

"Bless you," he said.

He bet it all on one hand of blackjack. He won. He left the forty out. He won. He left out eighty and lost. Now he had nothing again. Call walked back out to the street.

He asked for eighty more dollars during that night and lost it all. In the early morning in his room—dressed, shoes off, half awake—he watched the shapes breathing on the ceiling and felt a part. *In the darkness: Alive.* Was that something that he'd read? Was that Saint Clement? Niebuhr? *In the darkness* . . . Call visualized himself always begging. The scene was peaceful. *The Black Friar of Fremont Street!* Call said it aloud, and he smiled.

In the morning he charged breakfast to his room, gave the clerk his American Express card, and left. Sharon met him at the airport. He felt tender, seeing her. Carver and Lisa both were out on dates. "You look terrible!" she said. Call forgave her. She could only guess.

Over the next year and half, Call lost much more. His color went. He grew remarkably thin. He took on extra consulting work. He took out loans. He read as much about the saints and martyrs as he could. He spent time sitting in emergency rooms, just observing. He wore his summer clothes in the snow. His body seemed a foreign country. He dreamed of wings and pins. He spent more time in the dark. He flew to Vegas every chance that he got and lost his money, pawned things, took out loans, begged more money on the street. Call even stole.

It was out of his control now—he knew. It was all *beyond* him. He couldn't help it. It was like a fire, burning out of control. It was like a passion. He was like a lamb. Someone's dove! He was being sacrificed, being *given.* A life beyond this life was spreading in him, wheeling, wanting light. He was not accountable. It was love, this humiliation. It was self-reducing abandon. If Call lost himself in this world, he understood, he would be found—somewhere else; *someone* would find him where life was higher. God the Father! The Human Pincushion at the circus! Besides, he just liked to lose; that was all.

And of course he *hated* it too. He cried. He shrieked aloud. He beat his fists to bleeding against the concrete walls of leveled parking lots. He lanced his arms with bottles. He drank. He vomited. He slept outside with the trash. He landed in holding and drunk tanks. But he *deserved* the punishment. Call understood. It leveled him. It cleared him. It brought him back. His father had loved the Dying. Saint Paul, Saint Clement, *all* the extraordinary men had been afraid. History carried torches! The streets were lined with his brothers. Call was illuminated by love.

His dreams were like a gallery of medieval paintings. He took little care of his teeth. He gave away most of his suits to St. Vincent de Paul. His hands were almost always blood-flecked. He sold his eyes for five thousand dollars to the future of medicine. Carver and Lisa moved out and got apartments on their own. Who could blame them? Sharon seemed like Saint Catherine on her wheel. At the end of winter, Call lost his final job.

"Come to Vegas with me," he said. Sharon had locked herself in their bathroom, where she rocked in the cool and empty tub, back and forth, choked with sobs. "If you come. If you can come. If you can share this with me *just once*, do that and forgive. Forgive me! Forgive my sins! Then it can *end*. I can stop it. I can end all of this. I *want* to. Sharon: I *can*!"

Call heard her stop. He heard her climbing out of the tub. He heard the lock turn on the door. He saw her standing there: face streaked, hair stringing, looking ravaged.

"Oh, Call," she said. They held each other. "Call, I will!"

Call borrowed four thousand dollars at outrageous interest. All of his credit cards had been taken away. He and Sharon packed their bags. She was frightened. She, too, had lost a great deal of weight. She looked alcoholic—though it was only nerves. They stood at the boarding gate at Logan Airport, clothes too large, looking like prisoners of war. Neither dared to speak. Call was reading. Finally Sharon ventured: "What's that book?"

"Erasmus."

"And the other?"

"It's called *Pelagius and the Apostle Paul*."

"It's hard . . . "—Sharon cleared her throat—". . . for me . . . to follow."

"It's interesting," Call said simply. "Paul was right, I think. Not Pelagius."

They landed at McCarran in the rain. Call felt vaguely extinguished. Partly, it was Erasmus. The runway rippled, liquid and black. They took a cab to the Sahara.

"Palm trees," Sharon observed.

"It's the desert," Call explained.

They unpacked. Call's scalp and forehead began to burn. He took a shower. Sharon stood looking out.

"What would you like?" Call asked, drying.

"I don't know what there is," Sharon said.

The rain burned off. They walked the Strip. Something inside of Call seemed to devour his oxygen. He bought Sharon clothes. She didn't want any of them. "What was here before all of this?" Sharon asked.

"Sand," Call said. "Joshua trees." His ribs felt cauterized. "Cactus."

She looked around. Call could feel his hands shaking. They were both taking in much more air than they needed. Ravens clotted the trees.

"Are you going to play?" Sharon asked.

"No," Call said. There were brushfires behind his eyes.

Sharon bit her nails.

They had dinner. They had extra dessert. Call's mousse smelled like coal. They saw Julie Andrews and a young warm-up comedian, Bruce Carter. Sharon hummed. She smiled.

The comedian snapped and twisted lines out—all with pain. Everybody laughed. They had coffee and crème de cacao. Sharon took Call's ragged hand. It felt blistered. Call had rented them a car, and they drove downtown.

"So much light!" Sharon spread her hand wide against the windshield. It looked like a fiery moth.

"City of Sun," he said strangely. "*Lux—Lux Mundi.*"

They strolled on Fremont. They had shrimp cocktails at the Golden Gate. They drank dark beer. The beer evaporated in Call's stomach; it recondensed behind his eyes. They listened to country and western music at the Nugget. Sharon played some slot machines. Call felt suffocated. His spine felt to him like a brand. He could *see* all the bills in his billfold. Sharon won a twenty-five-dollar jackpot. She bought Call a Pony Express belt buckle at a pawnshop on Fremont with her winnings.

"I can't take this," Call said.

"Please," she said. "Please. I *want* to."

They drove back to the Sahara.

"Light!" Sharon said again.

"Light," Call repeated.

In their room, they made shoddy love—gaunt, trying to flesh itself around some sort of memory. Their bedsheets seemed extraordinarily dry. Call stayed awake, coughing. Sharon fell asleep. He rose for water.

He drank. There was an arsonist in him, spreading pain. Call looked out through the windows. He saw the city. He saw the light. He imagined himself spread and glowing across the sky the way Sharon's hand had been spread earlier on the windshield: pinned, only bones appearing, bones and a nimbus, the flesh illumined. What did he want out of God? Was that his questing?

He dressed. He left the room and went down into the casino. Call did not like the Strip—too much splendor, too insulated. He drove his car down to the city, parking it in a municipal garage. The concrete and steel hovered like a skeleton. It breathed the taste of lime, exhaled a calcium poverty. Crusty glass waited in the corners like mice. Call imagined his mouth filled with broken teeth—or pebbles. He felt at home in an uncanny way.

He wandered to the Horseshoe. He wandered to the Golden Gate. He watched the action. He felt strangely calm. He walked up Fremont, all the way to El Cortez. The night was cool; the desert, there—percolating through the asphalt, through the double glass and steel. Call smelled mud and sand. He played away a thousand at El Cortez. He saw other people around him, losing, but he knew that they didn't compare. Few had been as wretched as he. Few would be as wretched.

Sharon slept on. Call was sure of that. Sharon dreamed in ways inaccessible to him. And Sharon drew her lines. She had limits and boundaries—and he had . . . none. He lost five hundred more.

Out on the street, the light was even. Time, season, year—the lives of people, their futures, hung in opaque cocoons here, washed out utterly by the light. "The light," Sharon had said. Only Call saw the long larval shadows.

He lost nearly a thousand more at the Four Queens. He drank Budweiser beer. It tasted cool. His skin felt soft and delicate on him, indefinite, like a cushion of dust. Call could feel himself diffusing into the sun. He went through all his money. He got a loan. He went through that. He sold his rented car. He lost his profit in half an hour at the Fremont. He panhandled. He sold his suit. He sold his shoes. When Sharon found him, the next day late in the afternoon, he was standing out in front of the Mint, like an old, glassy-eyed pariah.

"Call! You'll *kill* us!"

"No—I don't want that."

Sharon flew away. She had the face of a madonna, Call thought, as he watched her taxi pull away, moving down Fremont. He felt great love. She was to stop several days with her family in Pennsylvania. Call phoned a man named Chuck in Gloucester, who was in real estate. "Sell tomorrow! Get whatever you can get!" Call instructed him. He gave the name of a party who he *knew* would pay cash. "Take a loss." He was talking about his and Sharon's house. "I can send a night letter. Giving power of attorney. Send the money . . ." Call named the American Express office. "Take ten percent. Make it fifteen! Hurry!"

Call begged more—dimes and quarters. He played it off at twenty-five-cent black chip tables. He watched and shuffled away. He begged more. Someone shoved him into a building: "*Get away!*" He fell. He struck his head. Blood soaked through his hair. Call remembered someone—was it Saint Francis?— dragged at his own request, with a rope around his neck, through town streets confessing gluttony. He remembered Mrs. Giornelli. There were feelings! There were disembodied feelings: Matrices of the thinnest wings! And silence! He gathered scraps—from unbussed trays at the Golden Gate. He spent the night in a keno lounge.

The next day, late, a hundred and four thousand dollars came. The house alone was worth over two hundred.

Call bought shoes. He bought a plain, gray-striped suit and shirts. He looked attenuated and pale. He bought a toothbrush. He bought a razor. He bought some toothpaste and soap. He got a room at the Western Hotel. It stared directly into the sky. Light spread through it like bees. Call could feel a weightlessness drawing near. He could feel an end to his own corrupting gravity.

Everything that he had, he lost in less than seven days. It went easily. It exhausted. It bled out. In his room with nothing, Call cried out to God. He begged for love. "*Lift* me! *Lift* me up!" he cried. "Father, raise me!"

He wandered to the window. Chrysalises fell, for him, throughout the light like sudden rain. And did the unencumbered self, then, take flight? Or was the street littered merely with husks?

It was hard to tell. It was hard to tell in Call's room, filled with light and nothing.

Slot Queen

They say she circled Nevada. Like the night. Like winter or certain constellations or rings on piñon pine. She came through; she visited, then moved on. From Mesquite and Vegas, I'd heard, in the cold; gradually north through Tonopah. In summer, Tahoe. Then down through Carson City, Reno—always tracing her map—east to Winnemucca, Battle Mountain, Elko. From Elko up across the Humboldts in the dog days to Jarbridge; Jarbridge to Jackpot; Jackpot south to Wells; then east again, to where *I* was. Just starting, working security at the State Line Hotel and Casino in Wendover. I had never seen her. But they said late in August, when the days were summer but the nights were fall, she'd arrive, come to town on a weekday, trailing her followers out behind her like veils, and dump every progressive slot in town for at least one super jackpot. It would take about a week. That was all. And then she'd go—moving again, like the light, down now through Ely, heading south again for the winter. It was an annual event.

It made me think. Because I'm just a person. I mean, I'm just a person like anybody: except sometimes I look at the sky; but that's the only thing; other side, I'm just . . . well, it's the way I grew up. It's the way Indiana was. And it was fine. I liked it. There was nothing wrong. It was Indiana. I couldn't ask it to be North Dakota. Or even here—where the sky is almost too large: next to these rocks, beside this prehistoric sea—waiting for the Slot Queen.

And James Breach is here too! And *he's* waiting. "For the right time," is what's been usually reported. They say he knows her. They say the two of them . . . but I don't know yet what is and isn't connected. I haven't seen. Breach is the racer who is trying to break the World Land Speed Record on the Bonneville Salt Flats in a rocket-powered car that looks like a manta ray and that he drives only at night. I haven't met him.

So there's me. And my friend, Harvey, who works the change booth. And Breach. And all the wire services covering him. And every day, racers and fans, who empty out of the mirages of Utah—some in vans, some in buses, some on silver motor-cycles and in private planes. The planes set down on old World War II airstrips south of town: near to where another man, Mr. Cooper, who I've also only heard about, is making sheet lightning in an abandoned hangar. Mr. Cooper's an inventor, and really *he's* part of it too—waiting in this desert lake bed. He's concerned with energy. That's a thing that they say. He's been caught in his own lightning more than once. NBC did a feature. So we're all gathered here. And every hour the Slot Queen is zeroing in, swinging closer in her rounds.

I was thinking about other things, though, when she came. I was on my shift, thinking about dinosaurs: how this whole area had been filled, once, with them and how there were people, even now, somewhere south by Salt Springs, who were digging—on a day that was like the bones that they dug for: huge and motionless and bleached. But then something bumped; something interrupted my thinking—a kind of stir, a presence, a sort of rush.

She wore bracelets. I remember that that was first. I was standing near the change booth and she must have been out of sight, but even out of sight she rang, like a game of horseshoes far away—the metal on her. "It's the Slot Queen!" Harvey said from the booth. Then, right away, she was in the aisle!

People moved. People separated. But all I could do was stare—because she was coming toward me, growing, down the long corridor of machines, and she seemed like all flesh and eyes. Flesh like white mud, thick and cracked everywhere, lined from drying, veined; her eyes not so large as endless, caves, tunneling back, tunneling back into a brain miles and miles away, out of which some hairy animal had crawled. I mean, I froze.

It was hard to tell, hard to tell things, hard to tell her age. She was dark but pale. Her hair was spread. I started seeing more and then more of her. She wore a patterned dress, white and blue; no socks, only a frayed pair of rope sandals; her toenails were painted green. And the bracelets—up and down her arms, hooped around the material belt of her printed dress—were like shields. And behind her . . . were at least a dozen smaller women.

They talked a language. I listened. The Slot Queen herself didn't talk yet. I'd never heard their language in Indiana. It had a lot of *clicks* and *clacks* in it, as if their tongues were made out of gears. "It's the Slot Queen!" Harvey repeated, whispering. Her ringing stopped. She was breathing. Her forehead stretched. Light was coming out from her brain. She was thirty feet away, stopped, beside a Bally five-nickel progressive reading: $742.54. All the other women quieted; their eyes like Mercury dimes. "Watch!" Harvey said. She seemed to be listening. Her nostrils flared. She opened her purse, took out a roll of nickels, and, on the fourth pull, dumped the machine on a row of 7s.

The women *clacked* and *clicked*. They brought her cups. She filled their cups with nickels while they held them. We issued her a check. The name she gave us was Annie Creosote. Harvey said it was because she smelled the way she did: half like animal, half like tar—like the desert bushes over the state. People called her that. She had taken it on. But before he'd finished with the story, she had breathed and moved and struck again and dumped a quarter machine in the next aisle for more than nine hundred dollars.

Some people are from distant places. I'm convinced. *She* was. I had lived in Indiana for twenty-three years, but I had never seen anything *like* her. She was light-years away. Once, my father'd lifted the axle of a Cat clear above his head, both wheels attached. I was seven. Another time, in Greencastle—in the First National on a Sunday—I had seen a woman in a transparent dress. But they were . . . Oh! And once a red bird had set down right on the body of a man thrown from a motorcycle near Owensboro, on U.S. 231. The police were there—but we had stopped to see if we could assist. And the red bird set down. I had asked my father if it was the man's soul, deciding. But those are the only things that were close.

The smaller women came with their cups for their quarters, and she gave them, and we issued another check. "Every day," Harvey said to me. "Every day, it will be like this—for a week!"

And he was right, almost. She lived there. She never slept—at least I never saw her. She never changed her clothes. Sometimes she crossed the highway to Jim's Casino, and stories drifted back. She hit machines at Jim's too. But we were all glad to have her. Like James Breach, the speed driver, who'd announced his run: Monday midnight, the very morning

Annie'd appeared, like Breach, she *brought* people. And we could see the sheet lightning, too, fluttering in the dark, like caged electric birds, on the desert's edge, just barely south. Mr. Cooper was active; *everyone* was, it seemed. And they were all giving things away: corned beef sandwiches on the house, pickled eggs, iced ginger ales mixed with burgundy wine. It was like a kind of dance or bonfire or festival . . . nowhere like my front porch in Indiana on the morning that I went away—my parents standing on it, waving good-bye; me and milk trucks, only, on the dark, leafy street—hardly anywhere like that. Larger, much more uncertain, for one thing, crazier.

Sometimes she would just go and *touch* a machine. Then the smaller women would swarm. They squeezed their quarters and their nickels in. And it would usually hit. And if she *wanted* a machine that someone else was playing, somehow it would get given up. Twice, only, I had to stop a fight. Generally, other players yielded. From the Tuesday when she arrived through the following Saturday, people seemed to know and hold her in respect. And during that time, we issued more than seven thousand dollars in checks; Jim's, I heard, more than two thousand more. She had a knowledge. It was like watching fire, or an enormous rock: you try but you know you can never stare to the center of it, ever—to the heart. I could love a rock, I think. I've thought that crazy thought more than once since I've come here. I could love a rock and be patient for its answers. But how do I know? I don't know what I have and haven't loved; all I know, really, is what I'm attracted to. So I watched Annie.

And I saw unexpected things—or I thought I did. Every fire has the secret of its own dying; and I thought I saw that, somewhere—way, way back: pain and ashes, that knowledge. Before the world was the world, there were dark birds, birds with heads like sea horses—I know; I've seen their pictures—

and I saw those birds . . . at the very end of her eyes. But then she hit another machine—and they went away.

And when she talked, when she said things, it came from really a distance too, from an underground filled with old bones and whiskey and flint. I heard broken stones graveling together and echoes. But she told us things about Breach. Friday afternoon Harvey and I held a conversation about Breach's upcoming run: Monday, midnight. Annie was near. Harvey was in his usual change-booth seat. "I just *know* he'll do it," Harvey said. "The Man is *up*! He's *ready*!"

"I don't know, Harv," I said. "What about resistance?"

Annie stepped nearer to the change booth.

"What do you mean?" Harv went on.

"I mean resistance."

"*What* resistance?"

"From the *ground*. The *earth*."

Annie smiled.

"What kind of resistance has the earth got for a machine like the machine Breach has built?"

"I don't know. But some."

"Not enough. The Man has *set* himself. He *wants* it."

Annie Creosote struck her bracelets against the booth. "I *know* Breach," she said.

"You *do*?" Harvey and I were surprised, both at once. I felt her bracelets almost around my head.

"He isn't human," she said. "He's uncanny. Do you know his theory?"

We didn't.

"His theory's—night."

"*Night*?"

Her voice was low and grainy, as I've said, unnatural. "Night. Because *then* . . ." She paused. "—We've *talked*. Breach and I have *met* and *talked*." Harvey and I had both been *told* they were connected. "In Fallon. Henderson. Other places. I know him.—Yes, night.—So that everything is back a billion years. This is sea. You and I are fish. His car is black light moving in the water."

"Is that true?" I said. I saw the sea horse birds again, moving, way back in her eyes.

She moved away. I felt bad. I didn't really doubt her. I couldn't. She and Breach were connected; I *believed* that. She was at the dime machines. She turned back. "I know Breach," she said. She almost whispered. She wavered. My heart startled, like an insect in weeds. She put her hand to her head. Something was happening, I knew. But I couldn't . . . Two of the smaller women came up quickly behind her and took her by the elbows and arms. They led her off toward the keno lounge. Harvey and I could only look at each other. We had never seen her sleep.

Shortly after midnight, she collapsed. I was off; Harvey was off; it was another shift, but someone came to the Western Cafe and they told us. They said, "Hey! The Slot Queen is dead!" "*NO!*" I screamed. I felt my head fill with blood. I felt Indiana going off like a bomb. She had just hit a seventeen-hundred-dollar, six-coin quarter progressive twenty minutes earlier, they said. It had been her biggest. And all the smaller women had brought cups. Players stood. There was cheering. The group working in the lounge played a fanfare. Annie ordered champagne. God, I wish I'd been there! Then, it seemed, twenty minutes later . . . she just collapsed. The smaller women hadn't gotten to her fast enough. So her entire weight hit the floor—all her bracelets striking: metal, wood, and bone; it was all her percussion. That was what they said.

Harv and I went out into the lot. We were both in pain. Mr. Cooper's sheet lightning was in the south, but we just both got in my Pacer and drove it back as fast as possible. It was like some Great Winter had come and swept and swallowed up the town.

But she wasn't dead! No. Something had happened; the report was wrong. They had gotten her to a motel room, called a physician in. "All *right!*" Harvey yelled. "Hey, all *right!*" And we both got drunk, drinking tequila sunrises, and listened to a group, playing, called the Wheelies.

Annie got better. She got worse. The next days turned. She got better again; then critical. Stories came back out of the motel room every time the doctor visited. We were all concerned. Breach came one day. None of us saw him, but they let him in by her bedside to talk. He was going, in less than twenty-four hours, now, for the record. Every day the papers carried articles. "What did they talk about!" I asked someone. But no one knew.

Thousands of people had arrived. The word was out. Slot people, women mostly, came from everywhere: in cars, in buses, in recreation vehicles. They stood around, half like relatives, half like gypsies, waiting for reports and bulletins— in corridors, in the halls and lounges. They all cared. We tried to get them to move. "This is a public place!" they'd say. Harvey worried. He made mistakes in his rolls of nickels. Coins slipped through his hands. "What will happen to August?" he asked— as if he saw August cut loose entirely from the calendar if Annie Creosote died.

But people cared. They came up and asked: "How's the Slot Queen today?" I must have had a *hundred* people ask that. Or more. I began to panic: *What will fill the space?* I was thinking. *What . . . ?* I even saw Indiana with a hole in it where Indianapolis always had been. I had read about the Bermuda Triangle—and this was some Bermuda Triangle of the mind. It scared me. Once, I'd seen my parents coming back from a funeral. It had been an aunt. They looked so tired, like they had gone to such a distance. I remembered my mother smelling of damp wool because she'd had to stand in the cemetery, in the rain. They hadn't asked me. I hadn't gone.

It was like their bedroom: foreign. Less so, now.

And we were worried about the people being a fire hazard, too—a security problem. Sometimes they blocked the exits, or seemed to. It was hard to pass through. The taste of living people was everywhere in the lobby.

We asked one of the original smaller women what we should do. She seemed the closest to Annie. "Get the Queen to say something," she said. "Get the Queen to write something down. And they'll do it. They'll abide."

So we did. And Annie wrote: "Go to Elko and wait! Go to the Commercial." The smaller woman, who took the note back to the others, said there was an enormous polar bear caged in glass at the Commercial. I knew. I'd heard. So the smaller woman took the note back, and in two hours all the others were gone.

The smaller women stayed: the original group. They took a room. Harvey said, "There are meetings going on," and I sensed it—though I didn't have the same feeling for what might be happening.

The next night, after my shift, I drove my Pacer out to the Bonneville Speedway. It was Monday. The last report on Annie was "fair." I was by myself; Harvey was off somewhere; he was busy—but I liked having the time.

Breach was going for the record at midnight. His goal was 650 miles per hour. No other human being in a car had ever gone that fast. In some ways, it was hard even to believe; Breach was just a year older than me—Breach was twenty-six.

I drove slowly to the parking lot on the Flats. It was eleven-thirty; my car radio was going, but I wasn't hearing anything; I was here, but I was also very far away. I thought of all the tollbooths, strung like dim bulbs, out through the midnights and early mornings of the Midwest: I don't know why. Wendover was a chain of lights three miles west. The sky, like motor oil; it seemed slippery. Breach *was* going for it. You could tell. The lot was swelling. And I could smell the salt— from the dead lake that these flats used to be—as I stood, with one hand around the CB aerial of my Pacer, trying to understand it.

I thought of towns; I thought of Indiana and towns there: Argos, Michiana Shores, Ora, Cottage Grove. I thought of Goshen and Terre Haute, Willow Branch and Portage. I even thought of Lamb, on the Ohio River.

The arc lights dimmed. They grew bright again. I found a place in the stands. You could see Breach's car standing out on the Flats. It seemed alive. A lot of people moved all around it, mostly in white mechanics' suits. TV equipment was up. It was pretty close to twelve. I thought about the Slot Queen *knowing* Breach: "I know Breach," she'd said—and then last night, Breach had come to her. I felt Annie watching from the rocks. What did Breach do, I wondered, when he wasn't try- ing to go faster than any other human being on the earth? What did Annie do? Was she always circling the state? There was a crackling, someone was switching on the speakers.

"*Ladies and Gentlemen . . .*" I started breathing deeper. "*In just seven minutes . . . Mr. James Breach . . . of Bakersfield, California . . . will attempt to break . . . the World Land Speed Record . . . of six hundred and twenty-two point four-oh-seven miles per hour . . . currently held by . . . Gary Gablich.*"

There were cheers. I was at the top of the stands, and looked behind me and swore bats were swarming by the cliffs east of town. My hands were squeezing my legs; I was at the edge.

The voice went on: "*Mr. Breach has asked . . . that all lights be off . . . during this historic run. . . . Those of you . . . watching from your cars . . . along the east parking strip . . . are asked to please cooperate. . . . Please extinguish . . . all car headlights.*"

Car headlights all along the line went out.

"*Mr. Breach will trace an arc . . . heading out and returning. . . . His speed will be . . . an average . . . over the course. . . . Thank you.*"

The arc lights cut. Darkness rushed in like death; it was only night. Crowd conversations traveled like rain. I waited—glancing off to the south to see if I could see the sheet lightning hangar flickering, and there was just a pulse; but I brought myself back again and paid attention. "Pay attention," Harvey had said. "*Tell* me." I was there.

Suddenly there was an enormous flare. My head caught fire. Then an explosion. It was all happening on the desert, right in front of me: Breach's car lit up. Annie seemed to rise like deep-stored mineral heat from all the igneous hills—and the black night was gelatin. It was trembling. It was hurt and excited and afraid and, without control, vibrating. It was real!

Then the shape of Breach's car left the light. It was all dissolving rage. The fish, or ray, or animal Breach believed it to be spread a wake of night to either side, pressing walls of desert hard against themselves—for just a minute. Then you could hear everyone breathe. It was like a three-second intermission. Then the rage, creature, *whatever,* was coming back, parting the prehistoric ocean again. There was a *Pop!* I could feel the back of my neck strain and tighten, like someone'd pulled a string. Then there was silence.

Lights started going on. Annie's presence lifted above us all, grew transparent. Breach's car was visible. And it was almost right in the stands. It had come that close; its parachute, blown out behind. Some people screamed. Everybody talked. It was history. The speaker came on and announced that Breach had averaged 676.577 miles per hour. Every spectator stood. I was shaking. Breach got out of his car and took his helmet off. His skin looked black. People went insane. Every television camera in the place was on him. I had thought he'd wave. But he didn't. He just stood there. He just stood. His hair looked white under the lights. He looked unnatural.

I couldn't deal with it. I left the stands. I don't know why whatever bothered me *bothered* me, but it did. I felt like I had become another *being* in just the last fifteen minutes, another creature. I was a stone on fire, a meteor. I felt so remote. Annie was dead; I sensed it; she was gone away from us. It had happened. I could barely walk. I was far from Indiana was all that I was thinking—*so far*; I could never get back. They would never let me back after this. I was the first car out of the parking lot. It was after midnight—everywhere in the state. I drove my car halfway to Wells.

When I felt finally calm, or almost calm, then I stopped. I got out. The night around me was unsurprised. I could smell all the mountain juniper on the hills. I could sense the rock. High up, in one of the Rubies, to the south, I thought I saw the phantom headlights of a car. A semi climbed slowly up behind me and passed, an IML. I couldn't see the driver. He would drive through the entire night, though. The rubber and exhaust pooled around me, like a swamp. He rose. He disappeared at the top of the hill. *What would Breach do next?* I picked a stone up from the roadside and threw it. Where did it go? Breach was twenty-six years old. I was twenty-five. If he lived a normal life, going faster each year, breaking his own record, then he would disappear by the time he was just past thirty. Where would I . . . ? People would search. People would send parties out. But he would be beyond their latitudes. I got in and drove back to town.

When I saw the neon cowboy at the State Line—the tallest casino sign in the world—lit up against the desert, I felt relieved. It was after two-thirty, and I went to Jim's for a beer and a sandwich. There I learned what I had really suspected: that Annie Creosote was dead.

I couldn't help it; I went outside into the night and wept. I felt hurt and torn. She had been in Wendover for nine entire days. They had said she called the women—just before she went, at midnight—to her bed. And they had talked. They had settled things. She had mentioned Breach.

Alone, at the edge of the highway, I thought that if I could

write, then I would write Annie's story . . . *only for Indiana*—
and I would send it back. I had the sense that Harvey was by
himself somewhere now too, screaming in the wind.

I wandered back into Jim's, so that I could have my beer—
and I discovered Breach was there. It was like a dream. Someone pointed him out. It's strange: I don't think I'd have recognized him even; his teeth weren't straight; he looked older
than twenty-six—like he was there for the second time. He
wore Levi's and a rose-colored T-shirt with a green fish sten-
ciled on it. He had a Coors in one hand and was watching the
action at the craps table. I thought, *How many chances do you
get?* So I walked over and stood by him.

"Hi," I said.

Breach eyed me. "Howdy." He said it nodding.

"You Jim Breach?" I asked him.

"James Warren Breach," he said. "Right."

I stuck my hand out. "My name is Neil."

He grabbed it. "Nice to know you, Neil."

I said, "I saw you break the record."

He said, "Good enough."

I said, "It was pretty amazing."

He nodded.

I said, "What will you do now?"

"Now?" he asked.

"Next."

"Drink another beer." He smiled.

"I mean next *year.* I mean, in the future. Now that you've
broken the record." I was thinking about Annie, too.

He just left me. He walked over to the bar, ordered another
Coors, then came back.

"Your name's Neil?" he asked.

"Neil," I said. "Yes."

"Neil . . ." He paused. "What are *you* going to do next?"

"Next?"

"Neil, it's your question, friend; it's not mine."

He had me. "But I haven't done anything *yet*," I explained. "I barely left where I *came* from."

Breach smiled. "Well, then you'd better start."

I pressed on; I got it out. "I guess you heard about Annie," I said.

His smile just died. His face grayed like pumice, eyes drew back. I thought he'd hit me, but he excused himself. "I think I'd like to be a part of this game," he said. And he walked over and picked the dice up and started rolling.

There was a VACANCY sign on Wendover, all night long. Reporters came from Salt Lake and from every region in Nevada. And they wrote the news.

On the following morning, all the smaller women, who'd been closeted since Annie's death, left their rooms. They moved in sort of a formation as they came together in the employees' lounge where I was, on a break, and announced: "A new Queen's been chose. It's Ruby!"

"Ruby?"

"Yes."

"Is Ruby one of *you*?" we asked them.

"We are going to Elko," they said. "Then down to Ely—and so forth. You have been so kind."

They left. Word comes back from other places. Ruby is Queen now. She's the Slot Queen. And Breach is getting ready, somewhere in California, for another run.

Now it's February. Some days the salt flats swirl so with snow that the whole lost ocean there looks to me like a troubled hole in space. The town goes on. The semis always roll through. We catch all the transcontinental buses.

I am gathering nerve. In March I've promised to go and meet the man who makes the sheet lightning, Mr. Cooper, in the abandoned hangar. I'm collecting rocks. There's a secret somewhere, and it's coming up. But we're all waiting, really, for August, marking time. Good-bye, Indiana—good-bye.

The Phantom Mercury
of Nevada

This is not science fiction. This is real! I swear. Real as light spreading over the desert, real as thunder in the Tuscaroras. Real as friendship: me and Ross and LaVelle. Real as any Mercury that ever grew to being in Detroit, its ignition firing, its spoked wheels making a blur, its radio blaring an all-night station miles away. Real as losing a nickel in a slot machine, or a dog under the wheels of a backing Bronco. *Real*—and such a mystery!

Still, I vowed I would keep it to myself. And I made LaVelle swear. I said, "LaVelle—whatever happens; if you and I get married or don't get married; if you decide to go off to Winnemucca and sing with that group at the Star; or if you go with Mr. Forbes to Dallas—whatever. Please! Don't tell!" I had taken her on my trail bike up Mount Lewis and we had spent the night there, "engaged." The sun, blood-red, was just climbing in the east, beyond Dunphy, and reaching toward our own streets in Battle Mountain. I took a bluish-veined rock and nearly crushed my left pinkie finger to impress upon LaVelle that I meant what I said. *It was real! Ross Haine was missing.* That was all we knew or should ever say. He'd gone *off*. Maybe he'd gone to be a busboy, down at Stockman's in Elko, like he sometimes said he would. But we should never breathe a word about what we felt had happened to Ross with the Phantom Mercury. Who knew? And LaVelle cried. And she sucked away the blood from my struck pinkie. And she said, "Yes, Jason! I promise! Yes!" But now LaVelle's gone. And my dreams are just about exploding. So...

My parents own the Owl Motel on Front Street. I live in unit 23; my younger brother, Richie, lives in unit 17; and my parents room behind the office. We're never full, but the motel, I guess, makes money; I've never heard anyone complain. I clerk seven to midnight, Mondays, Wednesdays, and Fridays; Richie, Tuesdays and Thursdays. And when my Grandfather Tombes comes up to visit from Arizona, *he* always clerks. We chip in. It really used to be fun. I could watch the Zenith or have Ross Haine over and we could both watch the Zenith. And checking people in, that was interesting. One time a man had driven all the way without stopping from Guatemala, South America. "Is this *the* Battle Mountain?" he asked. "Battle Mountain turquoise?" And I told him yes, it was; and he just lit up. And then I told him that I cut stones myself, that I had some really nice green-and-brown spiderwebbed pieces and a brand-new diamond micro drill and an MT-4S compact tumbler; and we talked rocks. He was a dark man. But now, of course, my shift is terrible. All the stuff on the Zenith is about Death. And Ross is gone. And now LaVelle. And so about all there is to do is sit there, scared really, wondering if the Phantom Mercury is going to come down again out of the Tuscarora Mountains.

I never want to drive. It sounds funny to say that, because

I always wanted to. I mean, I'd be going to bed in my unit at maybe one A.M., and a guest would pull his Pontiac or Chevy in and the lights would burn through my curtains, and I'd think, *God! Three more years!* Then: *Two more!* Then: *A year and a half!* Then: *November!* And I would actually *dream* about this one particular Torino, three lanes wide, with its high beams on, climbing through the Humboldts toward Sparks. But now—Jeez!

Some cattle went. That was first. A family named Pollito had a small range on the Dunphy side of Battle Mountain up Rock Creek. And they started missing head. Their son, Lyle, knew Richie and Richie told me.

"How many are gone?" I asked.

"Six."

The next day Richie said eight. And the next, eleven. I talked to Ross Haine, and he and I took our bikes up to the Pollitos' land. It was early September, dry, the north creek barely running. Everything seemed brittle. And there was a flinty smell in the air.

We parked. Ross had gotten a quart of beer and we opened that. We sat down by some yews. We knew something was going to happen. We didn't say anything to each other before, but we talked about it afterward—and we *knew*. We picked yewberries, rolled them around between our fingers and tossed them, and watched the sun fall somewhere beyond Reno.

"Would you ever shoot anyone?" Ross asked me.

The insects and the tree frogs had started up. I didn't say anything; I just threw about three yewberries into where it was dark.

"I hope I get to be in a war," Ross went on. He said it felt like he and I were on sentry duty. We'd both shot chukar and grouse. I wasn't sure what made him think of it.

But then . . . both of us leaned forward and looked up. Neither talked. There was something . . . I don't even know if

I can describe it any better than that: something high and far away in the Tuscaroras. And it was coming down. And it was coming down . . . and it was coming down . . . and it was coming down. And we were both leaning forward straining for it. And whatever it was—we never knew what that night— *increased*; that was the word we could both agree on; it *increased*. And it increased enough so that at one point we weren't looking up and away any more; we were looking all around us. "Shit! I wish I'd brought my gun!" I heard Ross whisper. And then we found ourselves looking up again—because, whatever it was, it was going home, up, away, *decreasing* now, ridge to ridge, canyon to canyon.

The next day Richie told me that three more of the Pollitos' steers had gone, and I didn't say anything to him about our being up there. I just found Ross.

We tried to agree. We tried to write down some things that both of us could say we'd seen or felt, or that had happened. We made a list. "Rumbling" was on the list, slight rumbling; we thought a while about the word "vibration," but "rumbling" won. I was near a slide once, a rock slide close to Tonopah, and it was like that. And there was a . . . we hit upon the word "fluorescent": a fluorescent glow. It wasn't bright. We argued that it could have been just kind of the after-sunset glow, but then we had to say that it wasn't; it was whiter, greener, like the light in Mr. Iatammi's welding shop, seen maybe a mile away. And there was a chemical smell, just *slight*. All of these things were just slight; it took us nearly three hours just to get the four of them down, to agree. But we'd both coughed at least once. So Ross wrote "sulphur." And the last item was the weirdest of all. I mentioned it kind of as a joke, but then Ross agreed and said that, right, his teeth had hurt him too—when whatever-it-was was the closest. So that was it: a rumbling, a fluorescent glow, sulphur, and our teeth hurt.

LaVelle and I were friends. It hadn't gotten physical yet,

except, I know, in my head. Some of the kids called her Frenchie—LaVelle Barrett—which was kind of exciting anyway; but she had a really nice singing voice and played okay on the guitar. We joked. She kept asking when I was going to take her to my motel, and I'd say something back and we'd laugh. But we also talked about serious things. Her father had shot a man, and the man had died, and so her father was serving out a term for it in the Wyoming state prison. LaVelle opened up to me about it one day when we were walking by the Reese River, and she cried, and I just held her and let her, and I guess that was the main reason for our friendship. Her mother was strict. She made LaVelle keep pretty exact hours. Her mother dealt at the Owl Club Casino (no relationship to our Owl Motel), but she always checked on her. Anyway, after Ross and I experienced what we experienced that first night, I told LaVelle.

"Take me!"

"Well . . . "

"I'd like to see!"

I spoke to Ross. He said sure, but let's the three of us keep it at that. So we decided on the following Thursday night.

We went up at just the same time. LaVelle had a horse named Tar (she was supposed to just be out riding), and we met her at a certain place, east on I-80; and then the three of us, on Tar—poor Tar! It was crowded—rode on up.

It wasn't quite sundown, so we investigated. "What if Mr. Pollito sees us and shoots at us?" LaVelle asked. I said, "I'll just tell him I'm Richie's brother and that we're trying to catch his rustlers. He'll be grateful." Then LaVelle found a rock with a long white-silver scrape mark along it.

"That's paint!" Ross said.

"No," I disagreed. "That's just bruised quartz crystals in the rock."

"The hell you say!" Ross, for some reason, got angry. "That's paint!"

At sunset we all gathered back at the same yew bushes. Ross pointed high to the north. "It'll start up there," he told LaVelle. LaVelle looked at me. She started stroking Tar's neck. She fed him a piece of sugar. Then it began, just like the time before—everything on our list, *everything*: rumbling, fluorescent glow, sulphur, our teeth hurt. Tar spooked. For a minute we thought he was going to run off. He shook his head. It must have hurt *his* teeth. LaVelle had taken my hand. It made me sweat a little. "Gol! What was that?" she asked.

The next day Richie told me, "Another steer!"

We knew we were on to something. Ross, LaVelle, and I talked. We wanted to see whether we could add anything else to our list. "Did it trace a path?" I asked them, because I sort of had that in my mind.

"Yeah!" Ross said. His eyes just got *large*.

"Yes," LaVelle nodded.

"Coming down—and going up!" Ross moved his hand in a kind of oval.

So that was the fifth thing on our list: "an oval path."

We tried to decide whether we should tell Mr. Pollito what we were up to, so that he wouldn't pick us off by accident— you know, shoot us. But LaVelle was concerned about her mother. So we agreed that we would just all try very hard to be careful. I went walking with LaVelle after our discussion that day, and we wandered into the woods and stood for a while and kissed. It was the very first time. I was very aware of birds there, for some reason, and I asked LaVelle later if she was. "Not particularly," she said.

Our next trip to Pollitos', we decided to locate a little more north and west. It was closer to the grazing areas, where the cattle were. LaVelle was worried about Tar. He had shied the last mile and a half at least; he had tried very much to get his own head and lead us totally someplace else. "Look at his flanks," LaVelle pointed. His flanks were jumping. "And his mane!" She said the hair was taller than usual there, stiffer. But I couldn't see it.

"Why don't we ride him back a ways?" I suggested. "Where he's more relaxed. Tie him. Then you and I can jog on back to here. We've got another half hour or so—before dark."

So we did. We tied him and left him where he could reach a good amount of grass. I kissed LaVelle again. She was kind of against a tree, and she pressed herself, it seemed really hard, against me and I let one hand slip down from her shoulder, and she made a sound that I had never heard before. But then we ran together, holding hands, back to where Ross was, anxious. "Hurry!" he said when he saw us.

That night everything happened—and *more*. To our list we added: "always just after sunset" (which we could have added after the second time), "heat" (we all agreed we'd felt a rise in heat), and—LaVelle was the one who pointed this out, but when she said it, both Ross and I had to go along—"music"; there was some kind of tinny or metal or something *music*. And that was the night of the first really great discovery: *tire tracks*. There were tire tracks in a meadow nearby where some steers still were. LaVelle suggested that they belonged to Mr. Pollito's pickup maybe, but working in a motel and being as interested in driving as I was, I knew they were not pickup tracks; they were *car* tracks. And they were fresh. And they were *real*. Again, I tell you this is not science fiction. Somehow a car had come down through that meadow. And not long ago! Also, Ross thought he saw something. "I saw something, I *know* it!" he said. "Kind of a *car* or something like that shape!" But neither LaVelle nor I could honestly go along with it, so we didn't write it down.

The next day, trying to be casual, I said, "Hey, Rich! How're the Pollitos doing with their stock?"

"Weirdest thing!" he said to me. "Last night . . . !"

"Lose more?"

"No, but they found one this morning—*weird*—dead! Lyle said it looked as if it had been hit by a huge rock. Or a *car*."

Oh, and one more kind of connected thing happened before the *true* time, before the time when we actually stood there in the yellow-and-almost-black light, stood with no breath in us at all and actually *saw* the Phantom Mercury. A Mr. Forbes came into town from Dallas. He stayed at the Big Chief Motel and not the Owl, and so I hardly saw him. But his reason for coming to Battle Mountain was LaVelle. He found her and told her that he had promised her father—who he knew very well and respected—that he would do all that he could to bring her back with him from Battle Mountain to Dallas. He told her that there were quite a few what he called "peripheral circumstances" connected with her father's shooting and killing of the other man. And that he felt that it would really be "to her best advantage" (LaVelle's, that is) to get what she could get out of the house here and return there, to Dallas, with him. They talked for several days, and she would report it back to me. She told him that what she wanted, she thought, was to be a lead singer with a group; and he had told her that that was fine, that was a good ambition, and that he would do all that he could for her. At first she thought the whole thing was just ridiculous, but after a couple days, she began to look on it, kind of, as a dilemma.

Ross got a gun. It was a .45 pistol, made in Peru, he said, but he wouldn't tell us where he got it. "Guns are available." That was it! That was all he'd say. He nailed a Clorox jug to a stump near the Reese River and marked it up worse than a keno card with shots. I asked him what he thought he would shoot at when whatever-it-was went by the next time. He said he didn't know.

Meanwhile, LaVelle and I got on. She asked me to listen to her sing. She'd bring her guitar, and we'd climb Mount Lewis, then sit, and she'd play "Leavin' on a Jet Plane" or "Killin' Me

Softly," and I'd undo the back buttons on her blouse slowly and when she finished, she'd lean forward so that the two halves of her blouse would fall to either side and she'd just stare out toward Winnemucca and Reno, west, and say to me, "Jason? Do you think I'm good enough?" And I'd say, "LaVelle, I don't know." But before I could finish saying that, she'd ask another question, insert it: "What do you think of Mr. Forbes?" And so I'd just have to tell her again: "I don't know, LaVelle. I don't know what to tell you. He seems short." And then I'd look at her, at her undone blouse kind of riffling in the mountain wind. And at about that same time she'd stand up and walk forward and press one cheek against an aspen tree, and then reach in back of her and do her blouse up again. She was making up her mind.

On the final night—I call it *the final night,* although that was true only for Ross, and even then not exactly true—we all told our parents we were going back to the school auditorium after supper to attend the annual Battle Mountain Gem Show. We lied. We left early. Ross brought his gun. LaVelle was humming. We rode Tar partway, but on the edge of the Pollitos' property, we left him tied and then hiked on.

"I'm planning to stand right where the tire tracks were," Ross told us. "How about you?"

We looked at him. He was carrying his gun. It was a warm night. It felt like summer coming on, sort of, instead of fall. The sky was that color green.

"Have you two gone together yet?" Ross asked us, out of nowhere. LaVelle looked off. I shook my head. "Geez," he said. "It's just a question!" And he pointed his gun off at an old gray junked refrigerator door. We heard our boots and LaVelle's clogs especially, pressing down on rocks all along the creek bed.

When we got there, where the marks had been, we stood. It was . . . I don't know. Except for insects and the diesel sound of a semi down somewhere on I-80 below, it was quiet. Dark was close. And there was the smell—I guess they'd been there earlier—of Pollito's stock. It made me want to be beside LaVelle, to touch her, even her Levi's, which I tried but didn't manage too well.

We checked the air. We looked up as far as we could into the Tuscaroras. They seemed to change their shape. I'd heard a story once about a cougar that was supposed to live high up in them, one that nobody had been able, ever, to kill. His fur looked blue. And somebody had started the rumor—maybe it was an Indian, maybe it was a Shoshone story—anyway, that you could bring him down only with an arrowhead chipped out of black matrix Battle Mountain turquoise.

Ross stationed himself in the path. "I'm ready," he said. LaVelle and I stood on either side, a little away from the tracks. The Tuscaroras got dim. The sun set. The tree frogs started. I heard Ross checking the cylinder of his gun. I heard LaVelle and myself, across from each other, breathing.

"We're going to see it," I said. I don't know what, even, brought the words out.

"I know," LaVelle whispered.

"I saw it last time." Ross picked up the low, quiet tone of LaVelle. We were waiting.

Then things began. Way up. No sound, but a greenish-yellow flare, like heat lightning. The first time not so bright; the second time, much brighter.

We were quiet.

Then the heat lightning or whatever it was flared again, this time down a ways, closer in. "I know," both Ross and I said together. Ross called out, "Touch the stones!" We saw him in the shadows reaching down and touching the stones in the creek bed. So we both reached down and touched the stones ourselves, and when we did, we could feel them shaking. "Gol!" LaVelle said. It was like the stones had little motors.

Then it flashed a fourth time. It was down now, coming down, increasing. And there was that chemical smell that we had all agreed on—but not just slight. I heard LaVelle say, "Jason!" I said, "It's all right." But Ross didn't say anything. I touched my jaw. I could taste my fillings, along with the chemical smell all along the top of my mouth and in my nose. Everything grew. I heard LaVelle making sounds, halfway between crying and the sounds she'd made the night I touched her against the tree. "Get down," I said. "Tar!" she called out. "Tar!" And then: "Jason!" Ross was keeping quiet. It got warmer. Then warmer still.

The glow was coming. LaVelle fell down. It was sort of that welding light. And I could barely stand up myself because of the shaking in the stones. There was an engine sound—and then another sound, like the sound of guitar music turned way up late at night, coming from far away, from some place like Maine or West Virginia on a car radio. "*It's a car!*" I called out. "*You bet it is!*" Ross called back. We could see the shape. The shape was coming down the creek bed, glowing, rumbling, giving off showered light, then crossing the meadow just above us. Ross started piling stones up in a dam. The shape went out of sight behind some trees. "Look out!" I called. He said, "Don't worry!" LaVelle was screaming. Then it broke through the trees where we were. "Get back!" I cried. LaVelle was screaming with every breath. "It's a Mercury!" I yelled to Ross. I recognized its grille. God, it was traveling! Then Ross's gun started, again and again, exploding! I smelled gunpowder and hot rubber and transmission oil all at once, and my own body, and, I swear, LaVelle's. I saw the Mercury go by us down the creek bed, and it was all silver and dented white, pitted all over like the moon. *God, it was real!* Ross's gun rang out, then stopped. The Mercury revved once, then entered some trees just below. *It was huge, man!* It was the hugest Mercury I know I've ever seen. It was more huge than a Lincoln even, or a Pontiac!

It was dark. I was sweating. The radio music was in the air, moving, traveling always with the Phantom Mercury. LaVelle was stretched out, rocking, making a kind of sob. There was no moon visible. And I couldn't see Ross. "Ross! It's turned!" I called out. "Ross!" But he didn't answer. I saw the light, saw it turn its oval and start up north, through a meadow, then begin to climb. "It's going back!" I shouted. LaVelle seemed in pain. I went to her. I knelt. She grabbed hold of me and held me; she was strong. She smelled like Tar. She tried to but couldn't form any words. I said, "That's all right," and I kissed her. She was full of sounds.

I turned my head to one side and called out, "Ross!" again. But nothing came. Everything was fading. The light was flickering up into the Tuscaroras. I could see it. And it didn't look huge anymore. It just looked like some backpackers with a Coleman lamp. And the stones were nearly still. And the air tasted burnt. That remained most, and the heat. My skin was dry in places, and wet in others. LaVelle calmed down. The first words she said to me, looking up, were ". . . the music!" I didn't know what she meant; I didn't know what to say. I kissed her on the mouth again. We held it. Then I heard a stone turn, down from us, and I tried again: "Hey, Ross . . . ?"

Someone was standing in the dark. I helped LaVelle and we walked along the dry and now-empty creek bed where the Mercury had come. And Ross was there. He was standing in it, staring up through the night.

"Hi," I said. I squeezed LaVelle. I wanted her to feel that I was there.

Ross nodded.

"You okay?" I asked.

He was quiet. He picked up a stone and threw it. It was a white stone and I could see it leaving his hand for just a second or two. But then it went out, like a candle. And we heard it land maybe a hundred feet away. "I shot the driver," Ross told us.

"Are you serious?" LaVelle asked.

"I shot him." He was straight-faced. "That driver's got to be dead." He picked up another stone and threw it; this one was dark.

We hiked to Tar. We didn't talk. He seemed happy to see us. We mounted him and rode him back down into town. It was maybe nine o'clock.

What happened next was chance. We hadn't planned it, but none of us really wanted to go on along to our places and go to bed, so we decided to go to the Cascade Bowling Alleys and Roller Skating Rink and skate a bit. So we did. LaVelle took Tar home. She said her mother probably would be mad, but that it didn't matter. Ross and I understood.

Inside the Cascade it was pretty wonderful, in fact. It's nice to go around in what's not really dark, but not really light either, with one of those mirror balls in the middle tossing off spots of colored light. It's nice to skate. It's nice just to have records on, too, and to be going around, just be going around and around and around *together*, with your girl in the middle and your very best friend from all your years in school on the other side. And to not be touching the ground! Do you know what I mean? Do you know what I'm talking about? I mean, to be circling and floating there in the Cascade Bowling Alleys and Roller Skating Rink with just *ball bearings* under your toes and heels is *nice*.

We went outside after ten and just stood together. I'll always remember our feet on the ground again in the dark. It had gotten cool. Ross was quietest. We said, "See you in school tomorrow," all of us. I remember. "See you in school," each one; and then, each one: "Yeah" . . . "Yeah" . . . "Right" . . . "See you." Then Ross turned away. And we watched him. His Levi's jacket looked like it had been chipped from stone. I hugged LaVelle, sort of. *Why weren't we talking? Any of us? Why?* And then I walked her home. The next day Ross wasn't in school or anywhere. Then, four months later . . . LaVelle.

I know the Mercury got them. Ross especially. I see that heat lightning high in the Tuscaroras now at dusk, and I think, *Maybe he's driving it!* That could be. *Maybe he's the driver now.* And if I go up to the Pollitos' meadow at the end of some afternoon and wait—for the rumbling to start and the welding light and for my teeth to hurt—then Ross will come! And LaVelle! And we can all drive the Phantom Mercury down to the Cascade and skate. And Ross will be wearing his chiseled Levi's jacket. And LaVelle's voice and guitar will be in the air. And I can touch LaVelle again. And taste her. And be Ross's friend. It would be better than seeing Mr. Forbes eating broasted chicken in the Miner's Room at the Owl Club all by himself. Or waking up at headlights.

In fact, I'm sorry that I was ever curious, actually. About the world and about the real things that are in it. I mean . . . why do people disappear?

The Last Las Vegas Story

The Kid was a boy—save his eyes that looked a hundred. And his hands were all chafed and alkali—so that he could undo a fist and you might catch a salamander, light-struck and running for cover. The world flickers and surges, it seems; it sidesteps beyond names. *Kid*. And there's delight, sometimes, in that; sometimes, not. Hands, then, and eyes—in certain lights—could appear prehistoric, but the rest was boy, young: twenty-two, possibly twenty-three.

He dressed in work clothes, just the slightest beard. An opal Stetson sat upon his head, but then "sat" got argued, since the hat rode like a hat tipped by someone picking a fight. Or any number of someones. Number of fights. He'd been (story went) around. Suffered his time. Not the things he said. In fact, the things he said made no sense. Someone else might offer "Evening"; he'd say, "Lost the cat" or "Seems like the wind." Or "How's it goin'?" another person might ask; Kid would say, "Taller than ever."

Very much, then, like his look, his words caught and spun; they left the road and cornered. He could put people into the air, like a juggler. But then, half a minute later, there they were, back on the ground, earth underneath. Nothing changed—at least not things people might account for.

There was always a half pack of menthols. Trapped in his shirtsleeve, tucked down in his pocket. There are Polaroids. He'd take one, break it, stuff the raw end into his mouth, light it, smoke the thing until it was only ember, pinch, throw it away. His lips were scabbed with burns. Which, somehow, made him look attractive—because he was just a boy. At heart. I think you know what's being said here. In essence. Leave the hands and eyes out. And there was a baggie, in his hip pocket, always, of ephedra. Which he'd remove. Take a sprig. Stone-grind between his fingers. Drop into anything—whiskey, Dr Pepper, skin moisturizer. He said there wasn't a complication ephedra wouldn't address.

There were initial reports. Sightings. Out to the West—most of them from near California and the south. Places like Searchlight and Jean and Henderson. You'd be on a break—coffee, maybe—or it would be that slow time—morning, midweek, no one playing—you'd be standing at the edge of some lot, under a fan palm—and the other person would say, "Heard a story out of Searchlight. This kid . . ." And he—she, even (there were women)—would repeat it. Then, couple of months later, another person would say, "Heard another Kid story." And on and on it went—that way. Stories engendering stories. Like weather. Up suddenly. Very reminiscent of baseball. Where stories start, circulate; hard to believe—sometimes they're more, sometimes they're less, than the sum of their parts— about some stranger, no-name, who gets called the Kid: They say this kid throws a knuckleball over a hundred and ten. And you try to imagine.

And here, at the eye of what you had to imagine, was misdirection. Distraction. Which is quite a trick in Nevada, given the Industry. But with the Kid: he would step into a picture, and suddenly you couldn't see; there'd be no focus. It was like being hit upside the head. Or like spilt coffee on the magazine you're reading: everything swims. Every word on the page is three different. The color of a person's shirt changes. Guy in some advertisement couldn't be more quiet: standing, hands in his pockets. Suddenly, his hands are out like birds, the birds landing, taking off; he drives you crazy; you can't think, and all you want is for his hands to stop, because you don't know where they're going. Maybe into your eyes. Maybe around your throat. Then again, maybe all he's doing is touching you like a lover. Maybe he's got a diamond or a sapphire. Maybe he's got a knife or a gun. The Kid could walk in and make another person's head circle so that it was like an osprey or a sparrow hawk. Like the whole world was an updraft or a downdraft of wild lavender.

Which is why you could hear the ruminance—everywhere— all the various brains in Las Vegas chewing. It's a thing that occurs and is predictable: the undressing of opportunity. And when that happens, when opportunity interrupts the silence and clears its throat, schemes fill the population like the second run of garlic in a small room, no windows. You hang around, hear—"There's a kid"—west of here, south of here— who's all distraction—expectations begin to stack up like thunderheads. And you know: whoever—the person, the Kid— will either use or get used. It's a given. Someone, in just a matter of minutes, is going to get upended.

Start(why not)with the early stories—just a few.
The Kid breezed into Sam's Town on Boulder Highway...

walked out with just under fourteen thousand. Nobody saw what happened. One person saw the Kid at the bar, four A.M., with whole fistfuls of clam and oyster shells—fossils—showing them off, passing them around. Three days later, he walked into the Gate in Searchlight, out with twenty-two thousand. Next week—Mesquite, the Virgin River, nearly thirty. Each case: he'd walk in, hands empty for all intents; an hour later, he'd have racks of chips.

"All these words came out!" one guy said. "All these words!" Others:

"He was laying all these bets . . . taking them off."

"Thick as smoke . . . he smelled of antelope brush."

"There were cards in his hand. They were in the air! He caught them!"

No one agreed really.

But everyone acknowledged: he was all feint and counter-feint, all distraction.

"I couldn't tell what he wanted. He was telling me things. Asking. Just sitting . . . standing . . . not doing anything . . . but moving."

No one remembered particularly good cards. No one recalled the Kid actually holding the dice. No one recollected anything in particular—four of a kind, royal flush—on the video poker.

At Sam's Town, the Kid brought a keno card up for eight thousand. When they looked, later, they couldn't find it. "He said these *things,*" the keno lounge person said. "They were these *things,* but more like questions—questions . . . except not. He kept pointing to the card, the board: thecardtheboard-thecardtheboard. I remember putting the template over . . . then paying. But I don't really remember he'd won."

The next thing you heard if you were near—*in* town, or if *out* at least with your ear to the ground—was about the messengers. Different ones. Going out. Being sent. Queries. Introductions. As was said: talent breeds opportunity breeds schemes.

A lawyer named Deitrich—who was a principal holder in three Clark County whorehouses—sent one. Supposedly a guy somewhere in the upper management of the Maxim—Hollinder, Hellinger, Hechtfinger, *something*—sent another. Would you be interested. . . . et cetera, et cetera? Could we meet and discuss certain possibilities?

They'll swarm anyone with talent. That's a fact of the world in which we live and of reality. You dig yourself up a dire wolf or a sabertooth—somehow the carbon count on the femur, because of the glaciation *whatever,* can predict annual snowfalls—you'll have the Masters of Industry and Government lined up, their checkbooks open to page one!

The Kid told the messengers: Go away, scram, fuck off; he wasn't interested. That was what you heard . . . from whatever sources: Pass it on! Still, it was all the nature of talk—in the beginning—all in the nature of rumor.

And then there were stories starting out of Laughlin. Eighteen thousand at the Riverside. Twenty-five at the Edgewater.

Again, the messengers left. The messengers came back, shaking their heads. You heard that the lawyer named Deitrich had gotten pissed. What was this bullshit?! Was the Kid interested in sandlot . . . or in the Hall of Fame? Word was: Deitrich fired his messengers and went out into the yucca and beavertail all by himself.

For three days, at any rate, Deitrich wasn't in his office. No one could set up an appointment; he couldn't be reached. Someone said he was in the county, at this or the other of his holdings. *Holdings!*—aren't words great? *Whorehouses!* Anyway, then someone said they'd seen him in Henderson with a redhead; someone else, in Searchlight with a blonde. He was fishing, obviously, with bait.

But, while Deitrich was trolling, the Kid, apparently, came to town and hit Sam Boyd's California. They said sixty-seven thousand. He was throwing the dice: throwing them off the table . . . then rolling a seven; throwing the dice up, into the air, so they hit the chandeliers . . . then picking off some number. At one point, his hat fell and scattered chips. Another point, his Rolex flew—over his hand—and smacked the chip rack. He'd buy the ten for a thousand, move it to the four, take it down, change it to a three-one-hopping, change the three-one and make it hard.

"Don't keep changing your bet!" the floorman said.

"I was in a catamaran today," the Kid said, his half cigarette falling out of his mouth and onto the felt. And, while the boxman tried to keep the table from going up in flames, the Kid rolled two twos for a hard thirty thousand.

Deitrich arrived back in town with a Japanese girl. She *looked* Japanese; maybe she was Korean or from Vietnam—small but everyone agreed: a beauty. He went back to his law offices. She hung out. She hung out at the Four Queens. She hung out at Binion's. She hung out at El Cortez. The Kid hit Lady Luck for forty-nine thousand. Mostly, this time, it was roulette. He had penny stacks, nickel stacks, quarter stacks, mixed stacks, black stacks—everywhere on the layout. First they were here. Then there. *Zip/zap, zap/zip*—he kept moving them. The ball dropped, hit the wheel—no more bets! The ball caught, like it had been hooked, on eighteen, and, somehow, eighteen was the number with his stack of blacks, hundreds.

When the news reached Deitrich, Deitrich reached the Japanese girl at the Four Queens. "Keep your head closer to the ground," he said. Two days later, five minutes after the Kid had walked into the Mint, she was there sucking on an ice cube at the bar. Maybe it was just a wedge of lemon. "Hey," he said and slid her an oyster shell. She just smiled and slipped him a pack of matches. When he opened the pack, she'd written something in Japanese on the inside. "Is this an offer I

can't refuse?" the Kid said. The Japanese girl took a long cigarette from a silver case. The cigarette was blue. She held it
out—between her jade-and-topaz-ringed fingers. Five different men tried to light it, but it was the Kid's match curling
the paper. She blew smoke in his direction. "Why does that
feel like it's going up my ass?" the Kid said. And smiled. But
the Japanese girl only ran a tiny comb through her mascara.

The Kid bought her a sake-and-tonic. She threw it down;
he bought her another. The Kid nodded. He pressed his pearly
Stetson down on his head. The Japanese girl put her mascara
comb back into her purse and they left together.

Rumor ran: the two ignited every hotel room in the city. Just
about. Fur and hide, camp-jay talons, screwbean mesquite
branches strewn everywhere! Word was: a room they checked
into at the Aladdin had an electrical fire. Someone said they'd
read in the *Las Vegas Review-Journal* that—whatever the heat
was—it blew the windows out. And anyone who saw the lawyer, Deitrich, during this time, said he was jolly as hell, buy-
ing fire-retardant futures. The Kid hit Jackie Gaughan's Plaza
for a hundred and four, Fitzgerald's for another eighty. Both
times, the Japanese girl was with him. Half the time she wore
green; half the time she wore silver.

Then, for a week and a half, the two disappeared. No one
saw them; there were no reports. Still, all that time, Deitrich
never stopped looking way too sure of himself and smiling.

Next thing: The Kid started appearing different places but
not playing. Alone; absolutely alone. No whatever-her-name-
was: the Japanese girl. Or maybe she was Hawaiian. But just
the Kid: just himself by himself—walking in, spending time,
leaving—hair combed different when he lifted his hat. Mis-
matching cuff links. A capped tooth.

He showed up at the Golden Nugget. He showed up at the

Sahara. He showed up at the Showboat. He never changed his look: work shirts, slight beard, always the Stetson—he was easy to spot. People speculated he was surveying, getting the lay, calculating. He was making a blueprint of the future with his eyes and drawing its map.

Was he independent still? That was the curiosity; that was the question mark. *Buzz. Rumble.* Or was he Deitrich's? Did Deitrich have him on a leash? It was hard to tell. And where exactly had the Japanese girl gone? Some said they'd seen the two together, sharing a Buddha's Delight, at the Empress Court. Others said they saw the Japanese girl putting #5 sunblock on the Kid at the Mirage, beside the dolphin pool. But no one would testify; no one would guarantee. And no one seemed to know, precisely, the Japanese girl's name. *Niko . . . Kiko . . . Koko . . .*

What *was* said, though, was that Deitrich sang. Everywhere! He could be trying some gaming license revocation, and he'd break into song. *He's got the kid in his pocket,* supposition went. At least the two seemed to have struck some sort of major, certainly-more-than-petty deal.

The Kid walked into the Riviera on a Tuesday. With an Electrolux. He plugged it in and waved it in the air, whirring. Was he there for the bar nuts—or was this it: the Big Time? the Big Money?

He unplugged the vacuum, shoved it aside, stood a couple of minutes, moved, began to circle. He circled and circled. You could smell his circling, feel the adrenaline shifting inside, pit to pit, like cargo ballast. Every pit boss he'd circle, he'd tip his hat. He heard one, gray herringbone, say to his craps dealers: "Steady . . . steady now; steady."

Steady: right. *Steady*: absolutely. Good luck! This is not a steady world! And the Kid was a cobra. The Kid was a magic southpaw circling a batting practice, leaving his shadow everywhere, laying down these little sticky strands of himself like a spider. He was like a kangaroo rat on mescaline. People began to clear their throats. Choking was that thick in the air.

And then he broke his circling and just stood—back from a hundred-dollar table. Blackjack. He didn't turn yet—in—he just stopped . . . stood. *Then* he turned. Smiled. Possibly. *Possibly.* It was hard to tell. No one was at the table. The dealer watched. The dealer was black; his name was Kenny; he had his hands folded across his chest. The Kid pinched the crease in his upper lip between his thumb and forefinger. He moved it around, the way a baby or a crazy person might. He winked at the black dealer whose name was Kenny. Kenny didn't do anything, say anything; he just stood.

"Fly on the wall—right, Kenny?" the Kid said.

"If you say so," Kenny said. He'd been coached. He'd been prepped for this.

"Wag the tail that wags the dog," the Kid said.

"It's your choice," Kenny said.

"Like my vacuuming?" the Kid asked.

"Whatever," Kenny said.

The Kid laughed. He reached into his pocket, pulled out a money clip, pulled the clip itself off the wad, thumbed through bills like he was inspecting fabric.

He moved in. He counted fifty hundreds, laying them out so that they made a K on the table in front of him, facing in. "Kenny," the Kid said.

Kenny nodded.

"K for 'Kenny,' " the Kid said.

"Did you want to play?" Kenny said. A pit boss, tagged with the gold name of Bill Shore, was standing kitty-corner just behind Kenny.

"What's the color of shoe polish?" the Kid said.

"I'll let you answer your own questions," Kenny said. "Mine

was: Do you want to play? Or are you just trying to spell things with your money?"

"How do you spell *relief*?" the Kid asked.

Kenny didn't say anything. He just shrugged. And waited.

"How many hands can I play?" the Kid asked.

"You've got seven boxes," Kenny said. He swung his hand, left to right, touched the stencils. "No one else at the table."

"Can I play all seven?"

"If that's your choice—fine," Kenny said.

"Can I play three?"

"Fine."

"Can I play two?"

"Fine."

"Can I play five?"

"You tell me."

"I'll play four."

"Fine."

"Deal the cards!"

"You want chips?"

"Oh!"

"What?"

"I need chips?"

"It would help. You want to play—it would be a good idea."

The Kid laughed.

Kenny nodded.

"So . . . so," the Kid said.

"Chips, then?" Kenny asked.

"Oh . . . why not?" the Kid said.

Kenny harvested the K, the fifty bills. He laid them out in sequence, lines, ten to a line—Bill Shore at his shoulder, double-checking. "Ten, twenty, thirty, forty, fifty," Kenny said.

"Fifty hundred dollars!" the Kid said.

Kenny said, "Five thousand."

"Five thousand," Bill Shore echoed, confirming.

"Thirty thousand!" the Kid yelled out and laughed.

"Five thousand," Kenny corrected.

"Eighty thousand! A hundred thousand!" the Kid yelled out. Then he started barking like a dog. "Do you know what kind of dog that is?" he asked Kenny.

"Can't say as I do," Kenny said.

"Bill Shore?" the Kid asked, reading Bill Shore's name from his name tag.

"Can't say as I do," Bill Shore said.

"It was a trick question," the Kid said. "Trick question. It wasn't a dog. It was a squawfish . . . choking on saltbush."

Kenny slid fifty black chips at the Kid.

"What are these?" the Kid said.

"Chips," Kenny said. "Black chips. Five thousand."

"You're giving me fifty thousand in black chips?"

"Five. For your five thousand in cash."

"I gave you five thousand in cash?" the Kid said.

"Yes. You did."

"You didn't recognize the dog?"

"No."

"It was a trick question."

"You said."

"So—now what?" the Kid said. "What now? . . . Now what?"

"Now," Kenny said, "if you choose . . . you play."

"Sir: don't try to confuse the dealer—all right?" Bill Shore said.

"Hmmm," the Kid said. "Hmmm." Then he took a tall stack of chips and started setting them in different boxes. Three in one, six in another, two in a third. Then he made the six—*two,* the two—*four,* the three—*seven.* Then he made the seven—*two.* And on it went . . . for nearly fifteen minutes. Then he sat back and seemed satisfied and his hands stopped.

"Are you sure, now, about everything?" Kenny asked.

"I don't know about roadkill," the Kid said. "And four-way-stop signs. But other than that . . ."

"I meant on the table," Kenny said.

"I'm not sure where the second fork goes," the Kid said.

Kenny dealt. Somehow the whole five thousand dollars had ended up at one spot. Kenny had an eight showing. The Kid had a king and an ace. Kenny paid him.

"What now?" the Kid said.

"You have to pull some of that back," Kenny said.

"Why's that?" the Kid said.

"It's a five-thousand-dollar limit, sir," Bill Shore said.

"What's that mean?" the Kid whispered to Kenny. "What does *It's a five-thousand-dollar limit, sir* mean?" But before he had finished the sentence, the Kid had five thousand, five thousand, and twenty-five hundred, each in a separate square.

"That's fine," Kenny said.

"What's fine?" the Kid said.

"The way it is."

"What way is that?"

"The way you have it."

"How do I have it?"

"Divided . . . "

"Oh—I see."

" . . . up."

The Kid put all but one green chip on the original stack. He sat back. Waited. Kenny waited, his hand ready but stationed by the five-deck shoe. "It's divided up," the Kid said. "Men on one side, women on the other. Light and darkness. Fish and fowl. Crips and Bloods. What are you waiting for?"

"No more than five thousand on any one square, sir," Bill Shore said.

"Oh—five thousand."

"Yes."

"Chips?"

"Five thousand value."

The Kid started stacking and restacking his chips across the seven squares—changing the amounts, varying the piles.

Kenny and Bill Shore both tolerantly waited.

Then the Kid suddenly looked across. To the bar. He pushed his chips forward. "Change these," he said. "Change these up."

Kenny and Bill Shore each took a breath. Bill Shore nodded. The Kid was up seven thousand, five hundred. Kenny gave him twelve thousand-dollar chips and a five hundred. The Kid scooped them up and slid them into his pocket. He headed over to the bar, where he'd spotted Deitrich.

No one knows what got said. Precisely. Exactly. No one, apparently, stood that close. But the Kid grabbed Deitrich's glass and pitched it, breaking the bar mirror. And not a soul from management or security made a move. They say that if the Kid had had fingers on his eyeballs, they'd have been around Deitrich's throat. Someone said the Kid shouted, "Birds gotta swim! Fish gotta fly!" and that, as he shouted, the lights all came on, hot, on the lounge stage—and some amped music hit—the Japanese girl, suddenly in a spot with a hand mike, singing Garth Brooks's "Victim of the Game." It stopped the Kid, it seems, short—from doing whatever he was doing. From whatever he was *planning*, probably, to do.

And Deitrich straightened his tie. They say. Stroked his throat. And set a bill on the bar. Left. And the Japanese girl went on to sing a set—mostly Crystal Gayle and Marty Robbins and Shenandoah songs. Songs like "When I Dream" and "Ribbon of Darkness" and "Ghost in This House." And the Kid stayed there, downing Tecate after Tecate, scattering little pieces of rhyolite all over the bar. And when she finished, singing the last verse of "Friends in Low Places" in Japanese, the lights went out; she stepped down from the stage, and they left together.

So that was it. Whatever the deal, it had been accomplished or betrayed, and the game was whatever the game was meant to be at that particular moment—vacuum or no vacuum, ephedra grounds or no ephedra grounds. The next day, the Kid took the Hilton for four hundred and seventy-eight thousand. On Thursday, he walked out of Caesars with a million two. Friday, it was Steve Wynn's Treasure Island: nearly a million eight. Some said the Japanese girl was with him. Some said she was nowhere to be seen. The only other news coming down Las Vegas Boulevard was that Deitrich had bought himself a new Infiniti. Convertible. White. Paid cash.

And for two weeks, it went like that: *Boom, boom, boom, boom!* Major holding after major holding, hotel after hotel: they say for a total of nearly twenty million. A thousand smoke screens; a thousand patterns of distraction. The Kid was Siegfried. The Kid was Roy. The Kid was all of Siegfried and Roy's white tigers and the Sonoran Desert thrown in for good measure. The Kid was the David Copperfield of the high rollers.

And then, as quickly, it just ended. It just stopped. No more Kid. No more Japanese girl. Deitrich totaled his Infiniti— coming back from the Old Ranch one night on West Sahara. Today, he walks with a silver-tipped ebony cane. You can hear him coming nearly a mile away—*tap, tap, tap.* And he never smiles. He just practices law fourteen hours a day. Like the rest of them. Sometimes you see him reading the *Wall Street Journal,* eating gravlax at Café Roma. But you have to be there at the right time.

No one's ever seen the Kid. There are, of course, stories. What *else*?! But . . . Someone said he had a whole chain of franchised dry-cleaning stores out of Toledo, Ohio. Someone said he was directing movies for cable television. Someone said he and the Japanese girl were doing something with foreign money that had to do with ATMs and microchips. But who can tell? Someone even said the Kid lived in Santa Fe and was doing huge eight-foot canvasses out of colored sand. Another that he had a university teaching job in Pennsylvania and was practicing neurosurgery.

And, who can say?! Hell, they're probably *all* right. In their ways. It's not impossible. Think about it! I mean, we've built a whole *place* here on distraction. Now you see whatever; now you don't. Read your history. Fuck it: more's the power, I'd say. And I can imagine the Kid saying it too.

Dealer

At twenty-six, Hatch had lost, or lost at, almost everything: a father, a mother, college, a wife, their baby, any job. And so, trying to break a streak, Hatch packed an Adidas bag and took off, hitchhiking, on what he hoped was the beginning of a change. Hatch traveled west. He went to Columbus and pumped gas. At Independence, he lifeguarded at a Best Western motel. In Cheyenne, he wore a white hat and turned steaks at the Sizzler Grill.

In early spring, Hatch moved on west again, taking I-80 out of Salt Lake City toward a series of towns whose names all began with *W*: Wendover, Wells, Winnemucca. In Wells, he saw that the road north toward Idaho led also to a town named Jackpot in Nevada, and he took that, riding with an Indian driving a lumber truck. Neither of them spoke. They rolled north. They passed a stretch of fences called the

Winecup Ranch, and, ten miles later, at four in the morning, the Indian stopped the truck and nodded for Hatch to get out. Hatch swung the door open without protest and stepped down. He watched the truck pull out and fade north along the only paved road in the nightscape; he followed, walking in its wake.

Gradually light came. The winter sun started up low in the east and Hatch found himself walking past foothills strewn with volcanic rock. Hatch wondered when the rocks had been thrown up on the hills. He sensed that his life, somewhere near here, soon would be different. Three miles later, in the town of Contact, he caught a milk truck that took him straight to Jackpot.

"This it?" Hatch asked, gesturing at a pocket cluster of three casinos and several motels and gas stations. The driver nodded, and Hatch took the weight of the small Adidas bag in his hand and wandered off toward the first casino, a sign flashing even with the dawn, off and on, off and on: CACTUS PETE'S.

Hatch had never been in a casino before. He had heard about them, read about them, imagined what Las Vegas must be like. But the minute he stepped inside, he knew he was home.

Something about the way light fell, about the smell, about the music—almost like an all-night radio station. Something about the sound of coins, about machines ringing, about the tin under-music of silverware in the coffee shop, about the reflection of ceiling mirrors, about the way people moved and stalked, about the way men in white shirts waited behind tables in the pit, about the dark wood on the bar, about the rugs: something about *all* of that made him forget the wind outside, made him forget his wife, the child, and the long paralysis of his father. Hatch was home. He put a nickel in a slot machine, won himself a dollar, had a cup of coffee, and left all the other nickels for the counter girl as a tip. "Thanks," she said.

"Who would you see about a job here?" Hatch asked.

"See the man? Over there? With the white silk shirt and the hand-tooled leather belt?"

"Yes," Hatch said.

"You see him," the girl said.

Within twenty minutes Hatch had a room in the help's wing and a job as a guard on the graveyard shift, watching the slot machines. The man, Randolph, took him twice through the routine.

"We'll try you out," he said. "If you can do it, you're on."

"I can do it," Hatch assured him.

"What's your name?"

"Hatch."

"Just Hatch?"

"Hatch."

Hatch loved the work. He would watch for people using devices on the slots: plugs, nickels soldered to wires that could retract them. Xeroxed bills on the Big Bertha dollar machine. Hatch had an instinct for gamblers.

On his breaks Hatch loved to study the dealers. He would watch them shuffle, watch the cards fan out, see all the hits dealt, watch the dealer turn his own down card over, take his own hit if it was necessary, scoop the chips in with his cards. It was all an image of fingertips, flashing like bird wings over felt, like small flames, like absolutely clear water: magical, dexterous.

Hatch bought some old packs of cards—"These cards have been in actual play at Cactus Pete's," the package said—and Hatch practiced dealing cards in his small room. There was a long mirror in back of a walnut-veneer dresser, and Hatch would stand there dealing first one hand, then two, then finally all six, imagining players. He would watch in the mirror as the cards fell, watch his hands. He was proud of them.

On his first day off, he hitchhiked to Twin Falls and bought himself a large piece of green felt. He cut the felt and fixed it with masking tape to the dresser. He taped six card boxes to deal to, spacing them in a slight arc. He had his own playing table, and he loved it, and he'd deal—sometimes for hours at a stretch.

On his next day off, Hatch bought chips and practiced playing with them: scooping in, stacking, paying. He was amazed at how little he had to pay off; how often he won. He could draw six cards to a twenty or twenty-one nearly every time without a break. It was strange. It was miraculous how the cards fell. Hatch felt select, he felt anointed and ordained. Cards turned in his favor, against all probability. He practiced "burning" the top card, a swift liquid motion moving it to the bottom after the cut so that no one could see what it was. Each day, for at least an hour, he would just shuffle. Finally, he chose the casino's best dealer and asked the dealer to watch him deal.

"You think you're ready?" the dealer asked.

"Can't tell," Hatch said. "Just can't tell."

The dealer watched for almost an hour. "Phenomenal," he finally said. "Unbelievable! I'll talk to Randolph." Then he left.

That night on his shift, Randolph came up to him and took him to an empty table. He instructed him, then had him deal. Hatch won thirteen out of fifteen hands. "You're a natural," Randolph said.

He had Hatch deal out all six boxes: "Deal right to left. Pay off left to right. Tap your tips. Slap once when you walk away; shows you're clean." Randolph watched Hatch's hands, the agility, the brisk presumption of his cards. In ten rounds, Hatch broke only once and, outside that once, never had to pay off more than two of six.

"I think I could do better with real players there," Hatch said. "I think I could cool people. Cool people off."

"Tomorrow night," Randolph said, "you start dealing."

Hatch was an instant legend. No one won. He moved quickly from graveyard to day to prime shift. There was always a constant turnover at his table, but at busy times it didn't matter; people spent their money fast and moved out, and others with new money came in. Hatch took it all. There was never any expression on his face. His hands moved. They were machines. He just dealt. He saw eyes, watched the eyes watching him, but he never saw faces.

His reputation spread. Players came from Elko at first, then Tahoe and Vegas. "Where's Hatch?" they'd ask the pit boss. "We've heard about this guy named Hatch." And then they'd buy five hundred or a thousand dollars in chips and play two, sometimes three hands at a time. And Hatch would go through them like a trout through rapids, his mind fastened somewhere in the light that caught the blade-like edges of the dealt cards. Once a man from Sarasota stayed a week, sending home every other day for money orders, playing only when Hatch was on duty. They found him hanging in his motel shower, choked by his money belt. When Hatch heard about it, he touched the various bones that made up his head, but he could not really be said to have thought anything about the man.

Hatch bought things. The management gave him frequent bonuses, and he began, very selectively, to acquire. He bought leather: leather shirts, leather vests, leather pants; soft leather, smooth leather; natural leather, dyed leather. He bought almost a hundred pairs of shoes and almost fifty belts. To walk into Hatch's room at Cactus Pete's was to walk into the presence of sweatless animals, a place of only cool and scentless hides. And Hatch bought himself a horse, a fine Appaloosa that he named Horse, but he rode him only in winter, in snow.

In the days between December and early March, Hatch would ride the animal out, ride him south. They would walk into the rock formations below Contact—the more snow in the air, the better—and Hatch would weave a trail among the boulders. He would think of his father, of the unmoving silence in any air ever between them. He would see birds in his mind, brightly colored birds, frozen, falling through unwinded air onto a place like seacoast, shattering. He would see animals, stiff and still and stone, standing in place, cracking, falling in fragments on a frozen ground. Then he would go home and, in the night, dream of rocks. His life had changed. He was not a loser anymore. He could win. And he could have a woman when he wanted. And he would always insist that she do everything.

That's what had happened toward the end of his second February. He had ridden Horse out into the snow-covered rocks at Contact. It had been nearly fifteen below zero, and he had stayed almost four hours without any movement, imagining deer shattering and tanagers plummeting, a weighted mass of shale and crystals inside his mind. Then he rode Horse back, took a shower, dressed for work, went to his table, and dealt.

Shortly after eleven, a woman took a place at his table. She had a look of terrified beauty that bore back far into her eyes. Hatch selected her. He watched her change two hundred dollars into chips and proceed to lose deal after deal. He saw her watching his shoulders and his hands. She had on a long blue skirt and a low-cut top, and, in exposed risings, her breasts looked polished, veined like good marble. Hatch finished his deal, brushed his hands once to show them empty, and moved off to the bar. She met him there.

"You're very good," she said.

Hatch nodded.

"Buy me a drink?"

Hatch held his hand up. The bartender came. Hatch pointed at the bartender for the woman.

"I'll have a whiskey sour, please," she said.

The bartender moved off.

"I'll bet you're a very cruel man," she said, her voice even. "The way you deal. There's something very . . ."

"I just deal," Hatch told her.

"No, you don't." Something like a smile appeared on her lips. "No, you don't. No."

"There's your whiskey sour," Hatch said. "I'll be back in about twenty minutes—if you want to lose more money."

"You live here?" She held him a moment with the question. "Yes."

"In the motel?" she said.

"Yes."

"What number?"

"Twenty-one," Hatch said, and almost smiled.

Minutes after he arrived back at his room, she knocked and came in. She took his clothes off, then removed hers. She kissed him and drew him to the bed. She pressed him down and stroked him. She talked to him, talked him up: almost a set patter, he thought. Like the stickmen at the craps table: "Number's four. You're knocking on the door." "Eight; eight; no field this time, but next time looks great." "Two; craps; two; a seven will do." "Coming out! Coming out this time." Hatch finished fast. She was nowhere near. She got up, dressed, and left. Hatch listened to the wind a moment. He could almost see it, like stiff celluloid. He saw a gazelle, inside the camera of his brain, become arterial with cracks, then fall apart. Hatch dressed and went back.

He started dealing. There was a man from Puerto Rico who had heard about Hatch in Reno and was there to beat him. He started playing fifty dollars a hand and lost seven straight. "Keep those cards coming from the top," he said. Hatch took another five hundred quickly. The man wanted to have Hatch drop the house limit: "Who do I see?" he asked. Hatch pointed to Randolph. Later, the man was back, betting one, two, then five hundred a hand. Hatch kept even, the Puerto Rican never winning more than one hand in five.

Hatch noticed the woman he'd just had, standing with a man Hatch took to be her husband. They stood at the craps table. Hatch saw her whispering to the man. The man looked back over his shoulder at Hatch. He saw the woman whisper again. The man looked back and fixed him with a stare. "Black-jack!" he heard the Puerto Rican say, five hundred dollars in chips sitting in the box in front of his seat. Hatch paid him off. "Why don't you bet it all the next time? See if you can win two in a row?" Hatch asked him, filaments of anger curling in his chest. The man took the challenge. The two pushed at nineteen apiece, pushed again with twenty. Then the man doubled down with an eleven and drew a seven to Hatch's nineteen. Hatch took his money back. The man started scream-ing, cursing Hatch in Spanish. He scooped in the few chips he had left and moved away. Hatch calculated that in nineteen minutes he had taken in seven thousand dollars for the house.

The man taking the Puerto Rican's chair was the blue-skirted woman's husband. He was dark. His hair was black. His cheeks were somehow knuckled, clutched with multiples of bone. He looked at Hatch. Hatch looked at him and at the woman stand-ing about two feet behind; he dealt and broke on a hand while the man was getting money out. "E-O-eleven!" somebody yelled from the craps table. Three jackpot bells went off in chain. Hatch scraped a piece of lint from the felt in front of him.

"Five hundred in twenty-fives. A hundred in fives," the man said.

Hatch took the six hundred-dollar bills and changed them. The man set a five-dollar chip in his box. Hatch dealt himself a blackjack, ace and ten, and scooped all bets in. He felt the left-hand corner of his mouth flicker up. The woman's hus-band set a twenty-five-dollar chip out in front of his box, then replaced his lost five with another. Hatch looked at the twenty-five. "Tip," the man said, and the mirrors around the pit seemed, to Hatch, to catch a brief light. Hatch nodded to the man, set the tip aside for himself, and dealt again.

Hatch had a four showing. He dealt his hits, turned over a

king, hit himself with a deuce and then a four. The woman's husband had an eighteen. Once more Hatch took in the losses and once more he saw the twenty-five-dollar chip set aside for him. He took it, nodded, and drew a breath. He saw the woman smiling behind her husband. Once more the mirrors over his head flashed. He thought of Horse, wondered if it was cold where the animal had been fenced.

Hatch took the man's five dollars a third time. The mirrors blinked. The woman smiled. The cocktail waitress passed taking drink orders: "The house would like to buy you a drink."

"Bourbon," the man said, "rocks," and set another twenty-five dollars out in front of himself for Hatch.

"What's that for?" Hatch said.

"Excuse me?" the man said.

"The twenty-five," Hatch said.

"Same as the others." The man smiled. He smiled at the other players sitting at the table watching him. "Tip."

"But you lost." Hatch could feel his right knee vibrating. He pressed his foot into the carpet beneath him.

"Win some, lose some," the man said and smiled.

Hatch drew a breath, twisted his mouth, set aside the chip. "Maybe," he muttered.

He dealt again, won again: twenty. "You can't beat this guy," someone next to the man leaned over to advise him.

"Lose some, win some," the man said again and smiled. He set another twenty-five out for Hatch. Hatch shook his head, took it, and dealt. The man took a card and broke. This time he set fifty ahead of him for Hatch.

"But you *lost!*" Hatch almost shouted. The man's wife had her hand over her mouth, maybe hiding a smile.

"Lose..."

"But that's insane!"

"...some, win some."

Hatch raised his deck as if to throw it. The pit mirrors

flashed and photographed him. People gathered. Hatch dealt out the hand, finished the others. Randolph came over. "Any problem?" he asked.

"I'm fine." Hatch bit hard, teeth against teeth.

"Sure?" Randolph said.

"Sure," Hatch said, and dealt.

Hatch won again. This time the man pushed him a hundred. Hatch leaned forward. "Look," he said to the man, as quietly as he could, "they're going to think I've got something going with you. I mean, why . . . ?"

"But you do," the man said, and smiled.

Hatch felt as though small stones were striking his chest. Everything appeared to be hardening into gems: tables, light, glass. He stepped back. The others were waiting for him. They were watching. Hatch noticed a man in a wheelchair playing at the next table. All around him, Hatch heard chips. Some of his bones Hatch thought he could feel slipping into new positions in his head and chest, realigning. Then he smiled. "You play with all kinds of people in a place like this," he announced to the crowd, those watching him, waiting. "Some just regular people—most. Some crazy. This man," he said, pointing to the woman's husband, whose chips sat in a stack beside him, "I think he's crazy."

The man smiled. Behind him, his wife smiled as well. Some in the crowd, Hatch's audience, laughed. Then the man pushed eight twenty-five-dollar chips forward to Hatch. The watchers rumbled. Hatch took a breath, bit, felt his jaw tighten, and took the money. "Thanks," he said politely.

"Pleasure," said the man.

Hatch dealt. He beat all except the woman's husband. Hatch had a twenty; the man drew an eight to his thirteen. Hatch paid off the five, then paused.

"No tip this time?" he asked.

"Not when I win," the man said, smiling. "Cuts the profits." Several people laughed. The cocktail waitress brought the table's drinks. The man changed two thousand dollars more into twenty-fives, a hundred more into fives. Hatch felt small flashes climbing his spine.

Hatch dealt this time and won. The man passed him three hundred, and Hatch felt another flash of the mirrors; he felt a muscle pulling, left to right, across his brain. Again he dealt. He broke. Again no tip. Hatch broke a second hand. "Lose some, win some," the man said, keeping all twenty-fives to himself, holding on tight, offering nothing. Then Hatch won: jack and queen for a twenty. The man smiled and passed Hatch five hundred dollars; Hatch threw the deck down and across the table. Watchers quieted. Others moved in. Randolph crossed the pit from the craps table. "What's going on?" he asked.

"Nothing," Hatch muttered, picking the cards precisely, one by one, from the felt.

"I don't get it," Randolph said.

Hatch looked at the black and red numbers coming up: four, seven, queen, six, nine, ace. "Nothing," he said. "I was dealing. I was trying to deal too fast, that's all. I was dealing— nothing." He held his breath.

"Take it easy," Randolph said, pressing a fist into a shoulder blade, smiling out at the table. "Easy." And then, off and across the pit. "Jan! Could we have more drinks at this table, please?"

Randolph moved away. The woman's husband passed Hatch another two hundred. Jennings, Hatch's relief dealer, tapped Hatch on the shoulder to take over. Hatch fanned the cards out on the felt with a stroke, brushed his hands, grabbed up his tips, dropping some, retrieving them, nodded to the players, and walked, moving fast, outside.

Snow blew over the empty highway and through the lights from the casino across the street, the flakes smelling like wet stone. Hatch lifted his head and breathed hard. Snow flew in, flew in sharp into his nose and felt jagged against his face. In the dark he sensed his eyes and mouth: not hard, not boned, but crushed and soft. He started walking. Boulders seemed to be rising up, huge stones lifting against the snow, looking like moons in the low air. The air was filled with undiscovered rocks. Enormous things rose. Hatch was crying. He and his father were talking about catcher's mitts, the ball sailing back and forth between them; talking about catcher's mitts, talking about pockets, talking about breaking gloves in, talking about the best catchers in the leagues.

Hatch drove his hands into the sheered rock at the highway's edge: repeatedly, repeatedly.

It was hard, back again, to deal cards with bandaged hands. In the first half hour, Hatch won only two-thirds of his deals; by the end of the evening's shift, less than half. He had eighteen thousand dollars in tips from the man; but the man was beating him regularly now, over the evening taking about three thousand from the house.

"Thanks," he said to Hatch at four when Hatch went off. "Thanks," his wife said, standing behind him still and smiling.

Hatch looked at the man and stared at the bones of his face. He thought of shoulders. Of necks. And of backs. He thought of a woman. Of an infant. An infant's feet. Of his mother's forehead, in the fluorescent light, in the kitchen late at night. Hatch nodded.

"Lose some, win some," the blue-skirted woman said.

"You're a good sport," her husband nodded in time.

"Hard as stone," the woman said.

"Tough as nails," said the man.

"Cold as ice," the woman said.

Hatch moved away.

Two weeks later, when anyone could beat him, after work one morning Hatch packed his Adidas bag with whatever clothes he could fit in and left. He rode Horse down from Jackpot, down past Contact to the Winecup Ranch, and left him, inside the fence, to be taken care of.

Life on the Moon

Freshman year I met this boy from Tonopah, Nevada. His name was Pierce. He was brilliant. We drew together like birds. How the world congealed. How the sky tightened upon itself, like some cobalt jar. "I love a girl from the ocean!" he would say—because the air was so drenched, really, with salt. And he would call me Ondine. "Ondine . . ." We would be cupped together in an umbrella, or in some cat's cradle of sun. ". . . This light drums on the pavement like oboes. This light here." Pierce loved music. It was what he wanted to be: wound in scales and notes. Pierce wanted that. And how close, how tangent all the possible universe seemed. It was for a month. Then finals came. And we went apart. It was frightening. We went apart, and Pierce went back and all that summer wrote me from a landscape of "sun and craters," as he described it, from a West so far away, where I had never been.

Pierce was so brilliant! His words . . . ! They came delivered to me at my family home on the Atlantic: words; pages of *words*. And Pierce called these . . . not letters but "Life on the Moon."

They came. I read them in a sort of trance. Pierce was so far away; what could I do?! They came until they couldn't come anymore.

life on the moon

june 7

Ondine; Ondine!

Where are you? Where have you gone? I saw you at the space center, at the airport, through the window of The Apollo. I was strapped in. I was in my uniform and strapped in and receiving only radio signals, but I could see you through the glass. And I thought, Oh, my God! Oh, my God! I am leaving earth! I am leaving the ocean and the salt and Ondine, to whom I could give a soul but haven't yet—and I am leaving.

You were so pale. You were so distant and so pale—in your very Eastern madras summer dress. Will you play tennis all summer? Will you go out with boys whose names are Matthew and Timothy and Jonathan? Sail? Hold conversations with your "adored" grandfather about J. P. Morgan and about Roosevelt? Drink gin and tonics in aluminum chairs and listen to the vague sounds of lawn mowers in the background . . . growling with the surf? Oh, Ondine, I hope not! Don't do that! Don't do that to me—just because I've left this planet and am walking with moon-boots in Tonopah. You looked so sad through the glass. You looked like half the clouds of May. Don't play tennis with Timothy! I will send pulsars back through space. I will call and speak to you through the radio-netted galaxy. And I will tell you everything about my life here on the moon.

I remember him climbing the silver staircase to his 747. I remember him pausing at the top, looking so lost, trying to find me in the observation room. I didn't know, until he wrote, that he had. I wanted, so, to reach out. I remember his orange backpack. Oh, Pierce! I remember the way his glasses caught the sun, making white tunnels only of his eyes. I saw the door swing shut and the staircase driven away. It was like the earth dividing.

l.o.t.m.

june 7 (cont)

For a moment I thought: I won't go; I have lived all my days on the moon, and why is it "only fair" (in my father's words) for me to be returning to that lunacy now? I served my country. I colonized all my hours until last fall: Why?

But then the engines started. I heard them. The air outside the window jellied, and you were lost in some wash of acetone. Too late! Do you blame me? Don't blame me: please! Don't! Ondine, now you are the tide—there where you are—and I, the moon. I will send all these impulses to you. Even blind! Even across blind space! There is life!

The cabin jolted. We moved. Up! I am sending you a gift of distance. That is all there was. Take my distance! Take my distance, Ondine! It is all I have. It is all I have been given by this rocket ship. And I offer it to you, always.

Pierce spoke about "orbiting McCarran Airport in an electric sky." He detailed his "module." He described his family—father, mother, two sisters—meeting him, as "sympathetic creatures." He said that in the "LEM" back to Tonopah, he was sick. He had underestimated the "Gs." *Everything* was metaphor. Everything.

It made me ache. It made me want to say: "Don't! Pierce,

don't *do* this!" And it made me want to hold him. So many
pages! So many . . . *thirteen* pages, in just that first entry that
he mailed. Toward the end, he spoke of "contamination."
"Ondine! without a cosmic gesture here, my system will be
penetrated and I will die."

l.o.t.m.

june 11

Ondine!

And what is this place? What is a moonscape? What do
you *see*? You should know! I will give you instructions.

Go! Memorize what I say and go with it in your head. Go
walking! Walk the beach at low tide. Walk and walk! Walk
and walk and walk! Find a place where there is no one,
where there is no other person. Where the world is sand
only and rocks and crusts of bones and the dried spines of
jellyfish. Only you must go at noon! You must go at noon,
Ondine, to this place so far, so far away. And at noon on a
cloudless day!

Now stop. Stop and stand. Don't move. Listen! Listen to
the heat. Listen to the choked crying everywhere. Listen to
the thirst. Listen to the whole vast, eonic thirst. Listen to
the gagging and the choking and the crying out of all parched
organic shards for . . ."liquid"! For sea! For ocean! For rivu-
let! For sweat! For spit! For sadness; for tears! HELP! HELP
ME!!! And that is what you will hear, Ondine, if you listen:
Jesus, God, Buddha, Planet—HELP ME! I AM DYING. I AM
WITHERING. I AM BECOMING A FOSSIL: I AM BECOMING PETRO-
LEUM BEFORE MY TIME. "The Sun! The Sun!" Do you remember Oswald shrieking that?

Now: Imagine that where you stand has been that way, been
at low tide for a billion years. So that every word you hear

rattles like the wings of insects. THIS IS WHERE I LIVE! This is Tonopah, Nevada. This is the moon.

If I were an artist—if I were a painter, I would paint *Dry on Dry*. *White on White* is profound, but not profound enough.

Ondine: believe me. I am being intimate with you. I am saying things. I am telling the truth—in my fashion. I am trying hard to let you inhabit with me, feel, see this place. I want you with all my heart to know what my life here is like. This is NOT the New England coast.

Can I be specific?! I know you are thinking that. I know you are wondering that as you read. Yes; I can.

The moon is composed as follows. Sixty percent sandstone. Twenty-five percent sand. Seven percent porous white bones (mostly skulls and spines). Three percent bleached lumber. Two percent electricity. One percent bomb-testing sites. One percent casinos and motels. One percent human beings and lizards. The texture everywhere is like pumice. The topography is pocked and cratered and uneven. There is no Time here. An early probe tried to bring Time to the moon, but it could not survive. Time died. Its remains are in a museum in Reno. Schoolchildren go and look through the glass at it and have no comprehension. Time is 97 percent water.

I went to the library and took out a book on Nevada. There were dozens of photographs of red, chalky rock. There were shots of ocotillo in the desert—and of sagebrush, and of greenish paste-colored open copper pits, and of the Lehman Caves. I imagined Pierce cloistered in them, in a gothic maze of stalactites, writing his chorale. Pierce was a composer. That was what he wanted to be. The chamber group at school had performed one of his quartets. It was thrilling. There was so much applause. It was when I met him. God, I couldn't believe: A freshman composer from Nevada!

I sent Pierce a canteen filled with water—parcel post. I wrote him back right away, saying: "But the desert *blooms*. Doesn't it *bloom*, Pierce?! And what about Boulder Dam? Pierce: I *love* you. I will keep the ocean safe until September. Are you working on your chorale?" It was only June. I had no sense of August.

l.o.t.m.

june 15 (excerpt)

Ondine:

I drank the water, and my sisters tried to cut me open for it. "Who *is* she?! Who *is* she?!" they asked. Ondine: the *greed*!

Yes, the desert blooms. But, like me, keeping you from my sisters, it will not give up its secret. I have *gone* there. I have gotten down on my knees. I have pleaded. I think the desert may be run by the government.

Boulder Dam: . . . later; another chapter.

My chorale! My chorale! I am trying. I am trying and try-ing. At school, back on earth, I could do it in one rainy day. I don't know. I don't know, Ondine; it needs oxygen. My father speaks of pulling me out of school.

l.o.t.m.

june 19 (excerpt)

Ondine:

More talk of no return. The space grows darker. Look up! Look up, Ondine: Can you see?! We are at three-quarters here on the moon, now. Three-quarters and diminishing.

Will you see my light go out? Will you hear me when there is only darkness and the mother ship has returned bearing only instruments? Instruments and data. Ondine: "data!" Can you imagine it? My ship will return, and you will go to the space station to meet it, bringing me a dozen tangerines, and they will tell you: "Sorry. Only data." Don't marry Timothy, Ondine. Don't take him to the pier in the moonlight—after I'm only *data* and the full circle of this satellite returns. I can give you everything I have. But I couldn't bear to reflect, at all, on Timothy!

What could I do? I had no sense what to *do*. I drew the shape of Nevada—trapezoidal, with its little nicked corner—on every blank surface that I owned.

l.o.t.m.

june 24 (excerpt)

They have hidden my space helmet, all the life-sustaining apparatus in it. I can barely breathe! My father talks of "transferring," transferring to the University of Nevada at Las Vegas.

Pierce and I had never been photographed. Oh, Pierce! I tried to draw his picture from memory. It looked like someone stumbled across in a book who you wish that you had known. He was all lips and forehead and eyes.

l.o.t.m.

july 1 (excerpt)

The commander (my father) says: Hotel School. He says we need to colonize the moon. He says I have responsibility. He says he came to the moon as an Estonian immigrant in 1937, that he had forty-four dollars in his pocket, that he washed dishes, that he did custodial work, that he prospected, that he built two motels—the Silver Queen and the Sundowner—both with blisters on his hands, that he has done it FOR THE FUTURE. FOR THE FUTURE OF MANKIND AND LIFE ON THIS DRY ORBITING ROCK. And for his second in command.

I can write music for the Center for the Performing Arts at the Aladdin, after all, CAN'T I? When I am head busboy there. When I am head waiter. When I am head maître d'. When I am pit boss. When I am director of public relations.

OooNDiiiiiiiiiiiiiiiiiiiiiiiiiiiiiiiiiiiiiiiiiiiiiiiiiiiiiiiiine!!!!

I called him. A female voice answered and said they hadn't seen him for a day. I called back two hours later. Hadn't I understood, the same voice asked again: he was gone. "What have you done with him?!" I screamed.

I walked out to the ocean. It was dusk and a faint spray was blowing in across the water from the southeast. I walked along the shore. *Pierce,* I thought: *Pierce.* I looked up at the moon—less than half now, losing breadth every night in the sky. It looked like someone had carved it, ever so thinly, of apple meat. I felt scared. The water came up over my feet. I put my hands in it. I licked my hands for the salt. The taste was close. I thought of meeting Pierce for tea in May at a sidewalk shop in the city. When I came, when I arrived, he was there first, waiting for me, whistling a Brandenburg Concerto.

Two days later, I called him, and he still was gone.

l.o.t.m.

july 11 (excerpt)

Ondine:

I am coming! I am returning to earth! I am building a rocket of my own. It will have all my own systems and my own power. It will be MY ROCKET—MY APOLLO. It will have all my own stages on it, my own thrust, my own landing gear. IT IS UNDER CONSTRUCTION.

You called. I know. I'm sorry. My sisters hissed: "Who *is* she?" I said: "I love an alien!" They fell like spiders over the floor.

I left. There is a lake, mostly on Earth, California, but with shore on The Moon. I went. It gives off oxygen. I slept out one night and saw the whole kindled universe from my bed. I saw The Earth. I saw its lamps on another shore. And I thought: I can SWIM! I can SWIM through space! I'll come up where Ondine holds a sherbet cup as if it were the orange wing of a monarch. And I'll wrestle Timothy to the death on the beach.

So I took my clothes off. In the dark. And swam. It was me. It was me: I was hurtling toward you—did you *see*?—like a meteor, leaving a phosphorescent wake. God, Ondine!— God; I was the Star of Bethlehem in *blue*!

Then something happened. They sent a ship out, an interceptor or something; I don't know what; I was tired; it was after dawn. Someone said: "What are you doing?" And I said: "Return!" And they pulled me out. I WAS SO CLOSE! They wrapped me in a blanket. I was so close, Ondine. THERE WAS ATMOSPHERE! I could BREATHE and TASTE. Perhaps you read about it. It made the Associated Press.

But now I'll construct a ship of my own.

I thought: *This isn't fair. Too much imagination. Too much pain!* I felt angry. It was the middle of July and I had not even sailed. I had cried and tried to do so much: understand Proust, see Nevada—like a rock in my hand. I had ached for Pierce in all his luminous remoteness. But I felt bruised. "THERE IS NO TIMOTHY!" I wrote back. I didn't even sign the letter. I wanted to add: "When you swim across Lake Tahoe in the dark, you hold my heart in your teeth!" I called a friend, and we went together for a week to the mountains.

We stayed two days. My friend was not my friend. Every night the moon was full and the clouds blowing across it looked like scorched rags. Pierce had never *wanted* to hurt me—I knew that. He had never wanted to ". . . try me out . . . see what I might be worth." It was just, with Pierce, that he had a voice, and that he needed to use it, that he wanted to make sounds with it that would, he hoped, create something large and spatial, like a song, like a globe, like his music. And it was only that he was *lost* in that. He had never, ever, wanted to be *cruel*.

I found the nearest town and took a bus back, alone. The bus traveled through dense and neutral air. There were five envelopes waiting for me. I wrote Pierce: "Pierce, I love you! It's all right, if you have to, *swim* to me. Timothy is dead." Then I opened the envelopes.

l.o.t.m.

july 14 (excerpt)

I saw a picture of the inside of my chest. It's a chamber! We could sit there in the glow of what the doctor here calls *leucocytes*. I could write chamber music for you. The picture focuses mainly on my lungs. Should I have a 3 x 5 glossy made and mail it?

l.o.t.m.

july 15 (excerpt)

They say I have a terrible fever. It is the first time any of my family have ever paid attention to that.

l.o.t.m.

july 18 (excerpt)

Can you see how my handwriting shakes? It's the revving of my engines. It's my own power.

They have taken me to Sunrise Hospital in Las Vegas. The address here is: 3186 South Maryland Parkway (702-731-8000); room 542. I am being helped here. They have all sorts of instruments. Sunrise Hospital—on The Moon. Can you imagine it?! I was taken from the SUNDOWNER Motel to the SUNRISE Hospital! I tell all the nurses that this must be a subversive place. I ask them if they are double agents, because if this is SUNRISE then it must be MOON-DOWN. It must be working to make the MOON FALL.

But if the moon falls . . . and I am *on* it . . . what will happen?

Work the tides! Work the tides hard, Ondine! Then I will fall into the Atlantic right beside you. And I will float to you, at dawn, like a white bridegroom to my bed.

So far! So far! So far! Oh, sweet Jesus!

l.o.t.m.

july 22

Ondine:

There has been a scene. My father visited me. His face looked tortured. He said, "This death thing." He said it several times. "This death thing of yours," he said. And "suicide." He thinks my trying to swim across the heavens to you was an "attempt at suicide." He shouted: "Don't you realize—that with this death thing of yours you are going to pull everything I've *built* here, working like an animal, down like *rubble*?!!"

"Working like an animal." God. I felt so sorry for him.

I looked at him. I was very rational. You understand, don't you, Ondine, that I can be rational—deliberate, clear, very methodic. There is absolutely no pleasure for me, no thrill at all in being rational. But it is not an anathema.

I said: "You feel deeply about what you have done. You have come to a desolated place, impoverished from another country, and you have given great amounts of your energy to create habitation and, in terms of your family, to provide. Is that right?"

He said he would not have used the words that I used, but that, "Yes": that was essentially right.

"And you have done it, for the most part, alone."

He said he "saw what I was trying to do."

I said of course he saw—because I was being logical and the logic was true: He felt as deeply as he did because he had done something considerable and done it under his own power. Was it right, then, for him to try to usurp that same depth of feeling from me?

"Don't use words like 'usurp'!"

The tortured look never left his face. There are tortured citizens on The Moon, Ondine. *Know* that. Not everyone here is insensitive or of a military mind. He said that what I was trying to say was not the same, but that I was twisting things and that I would see the difference.

But of course I was *not* twisting things, not in any way. The reasoning was perfect. Again, I want you too, as well as my

father, to understand this—because I love you both so very
dearly: I am not lost to rational thinking. I do it. And I do it
very well. . . . I can't *act* on it. Which creates a tangible
dilemma. I can only *act* on my *passions,* on my fever. But
neither of you should ever think that I am only some satellite, lost to the normal human race.

I read Pierce's entry of July 22nd several times. I felt stunned.
I had told a girlfriend, earlier in the summer, that I have "fallen
in love this Spring with a mad composer" and that "it was
beautiful." What rubbish! What betrayal! What giddiness the
whole exchange was!

What did I *want* out of Pierce? What did I *want* out of
loving him? Out of having that love of him returned? Who
did I think I was? What was I angling for?

I walked the shore again—an entire afternoon. The tide
was sinking away from me, leaving foam and scraps and offal
on the sand. The Atlantic terns were scavenging. "Ondine!"
Who *was* Ondine? She was a water spirit who, if she married
a mortal and bore a child, then received a soul. But was I
really from the water—Pierce's vision of me? Or did I *feed*
from it?

I went to where I knew the fishermen would be unloading
their boats in the late afternoon. I watched them hoist their
nets out of the hold and swing them over to the pier for unloading. I saw the light glinting from their eyes. I saw salt
mingled in their beards. I saw them touch and handle the
fish. I saw the bluefish and flounder. I saw the living that
they chose, all the lovely freedom and danger. That night I
wrote it all to Pierce, no embellishing, simply what I had done,
a description.

No letters came from him for a week.

I called Sunrise Hospital. "That patient is unable to receive phone calls," I was told. *Oh, not again!* I thought. *Not
still further.*

I spent two more days very close to the sea. "Where do you *go* when you go out all day alone?" my mother asked. I said, "Approaching someone." She said, "It seems morbid."

Could I marry Pierce—really? Could our worlds have children?

I called Sunrise Hospital again. I received the same answer. *Why* was he unable to receive phone calls? I demanded. *Why?!* I felt abandoned by an enormous sea beyond the planet. Even the phone seemed to sail away. "That patient is listed in a coma," the telephone receptionist said.

Sweet, sweet, Jesus! This young man that I loved and needed now, really desperately, to talk to was in a coma on The Moon!! Where was I?

I drove seventy miles to an airport. Planes rose up and fell like ashes. Should I take one? Could I? God, I hated them! I would beat my fists against them for all the white awful lines of distance that they drew if I could. Could I buy a ticket to Pierce? Would a ticket *take* me?

The next morning, another envelope came.

l.o.t.m.

august 4 (excerpt)

Ondine:

If you've tried to reach me here, then you must be worried. I think too much of myself. The word is that I'm in a coma. But I'm not. It's all theatre. There is *time* here, Ondine, at the Sunrise. And so I'm storing it. I am monitored, head and wrist. My friend, Thomas, the orderly, is in collusion. And I am whispering, and he is writing this.

l.o.t.m.

august 7 (excerpt)

My room is in the northwest corner of the Sunrise. There is a lot of glass. At night, even monitored and prone, I can see electricity in the sky. There is a sign: STARDUST . . . STARDUST. The galaxy advertises itself! I am on the fringes of an electromagnetic field. A discrete locus. No other spot in the universe is like it. Imagine Death, Ondine, resurrected in Neon, and you have it.

Also I can see the signal lights of other rockets, rising and falling from McCarran Airport. It gives me heart. I think: There is passage!

l.o.t.m.

august 11 (excerpt)

Yesterday my parents came and stood by my bed. They believed me to be, still, in a coma. They have done this often during my "removal." I have listened to them. It's been illuminating. This day, my mother said: "He seemed happy at first."

My father said: "He looked awful."

My mother said: "But he was *tanned*. From the *ocean*."

My father said: "He was thin and shook."

My mother said: "But that's Pierce. Pierce is thin."

My father said: "Pierce never shook."

"I've vibrated," I said, my eyes still shut on the bed. Some kind of impatience triggered it. I let my eyes slip open. "I've vibrated all my life," I went on. "I've always vibrated. It's incredible that you've never noticed it."

"You son of a bitch!" my father said to me.

"Karl . . ." my mother said.

"You weakling! You coward!" He ripped all the monitor cords from their tape. He slapped my face. I kicked his chest. Several hospital staff arrived and, with my mother, stopped him. Part of me regrets their intercession. *Would he have killed me? Would he have killed me?* I really wonder that.

They brought me home. That night we had a "restrained discussion." It ended when my father said, "When you demonstrate to me that you are *capable of supporting yourself,* of existing *independent of all other support*; when you show me that you don't need to be saved or sheltered or nursed— then *you can go back to that other place,* with my blessings!"

ALL RIGHT!! ALL RIGHT!!

Again, the envelopes stopped. This time it was close to two weeks. I couldn't call Nevada. I didn't dare. Something warned me. My breath felt like it was being kept in a safety deposit vault in my chest. The sky seemed stretched thinner than it had ever been. Finally a letter arrived. It was addressed in a different hand than Pierce's. It was postmarked Tonopah.

August 23

Dear Sarah:

I got your name and address from your stationery. Someone must write you this. Pierce, I know, would have wanted it.

Five days ago, Pierce was found in the desert. He had left home the morning after he'd been brought back to our parents' from Sunrise Hospital. He was suffering from exposure. He'd been living there, apparently, without any food or water or clothes. And when they found him—isn't life strange?—he was rooted staring only at the sky: dehydrated, badly burned. His eyes, unlubricated, were open all the time. He had no moisture in his voice. "His mind is blanched," is something I think I heard the doctor say. It's so strange, Sarah. We have no comprehension of it. So he's in a place now, resting. We have no sense whether he will ever return.

What is hardest for us all to understand is—there were rocks thirty feet away, a sort of cave, an overhang. He could have easily sought shelter in it. Moonbirds had, "poorwills," and they were flitting in and out of the lava crevices, flicking their scissor-tails. Also there was barrel cactus that he could have cut open for water—he knew how. He could have had shelter and life support, but he chose neither. It's beyond us.

I am sending you, in a separate larger envelope, the composition that he was working out there in the desert in the sun. There are twelve music-lined composition pages. It appears to be a chorale. On the first page he had written "for Ondine."

I am sorry to be writing you this. Someone had to. He refused to talk with any of us about you. But I'm sure he was in love. Perhaps someday we'll meet you. Still, the East seems far away. Please, if you know anything that would help us understand this terrible thing that Pierce has done to himself, write and help us because we can't.

It was signed by Pierce's older sister, Lyndie.

I needed water. I went outside. I walked along the shore again as I had so many times that summer. There was a light Atlantic rain. It was the only thing, I think, that saved me from some kind of quite unnatural fury.

The tide was coming in. I was unconscious of it—until, that is, I felt it swirling around my thighs. I stopped.

"Oh, Pierce!" I cried. How many times that summer had I uttered those words to the enormous sea. Pierce was wrong: I *knew* that, standing there in the tide. The desert *does* bloom, and Pierce was wrong. He was lost *inside* himself and flailing. Still I felt that *someday* . . . from someplace, somewhere . . . there would be this song. I could never have married him, I think that's true. I could never have stayed forever with him and still lived my life. But, still, I wept. I wept for Pierce. And for the sea I stood in and for the orbiting moon: *all* those that have no choice but to obey their forces.

My God, I wept.

Who I Am Is

Who I am is: You're staying at the MGM Grand, and it's between late May and early September and you're by the pool on your chaise with something that's got gin or vodka or sherbet in it and the page girl over the PA keeps saying: *"Mr. Leland Hetchgar: Telephone, please! Mr. Leland Hetchgar,"* and then again, five minutes later: *"Mr. Leland Hetchgar: Long distance!"* Every five minutes or so, it repeats. You're there. And I'm being paged: *"Mr. Leland Hetchgar!"* And you're wondering who the hell I am. Well, that's who. That's me. I'm him. I'm the guy who does business by the pool at least five months a year. I'm Lee Hetchgar.

O.K.: The first call's Champ Festnick and he's staying at the Trop and he's making noise. "Lee!" he says, and then he asks where I was last night, why wasn't I over at the Trop when he had a twenty-two-minute hand and rolled fours and

107

tens back to back and then back again and made all his hard numbers? Where? What could I have been thinking? And then he tells me, "People were going crazy!" He's loud. The telephone sounds like it's got dogs barking in it. I watch a kid do a sloppy half-gainer off the low board. He breaks in pieces against the sun. Cyndie, one of the pool girls, brings me crushed ice and tonic. "Champ," I say. I tip Cyndie. She walks away. Her feet evaporate on the walk. "Champ: The Trop's a grind joint! I don't care if a hand lasts *an hour and a half* at the Trop—I wouldn't be there. A hundred and thirty thou isn't worth sending my clothes out to get the Trop dry-cleaned out of them, brushing and rebrushing my teeth." "Hey!" Champ says. "Hey, you're talking about *me*." "Your choice," I tell him. We schedule golf. Champ's got a left arm that's about an inch shorter than his right, but he putts well. I hang up. There's a girl I've been watching work the pool for three days, skimming purses and beach robes when people leave them unattended to swim. "You want my watch?" I say. She cuts out.

Long distance, the first time, it's Sy Lakeland from Chicago. He's talking booze and he's talking synthetic hair. Some kid is trying to drown his brother out at about the seven-foot marker. The father comes. He tries to discuss Cain and Abel. Ideas make more violence than violence. Sy is talking quantities he doesn't even understand. He's trying to con me about distribution: "Listen, Lee . . . !" I hold the back of my hand out in front of me and try to measure the sun. I figure: one hundred and three. "*Lee* . . . !" he says. I ask Sy shotgun questions. He gropes. I ask where's his data. I ask percentages. I ask about patents. I ask for—"Come on, Sy, *quick*; you should *have* these"—three-year projections. I destroy him. I eat him up. He's got pistachio nut shells suddenly in his throat. He can't talk. I thank him just the same; I've got better things. I look up. I see a raven and a gull near the tennis courts. The raven seems to swallow a discarded ball.

Booze I mentioned; also synthetic hair. What else? I'm talking current, you understand; I'm talking *of the moment*. Things change. There's a convention of doctors here from New England, for example, and I'm thinking a line of radiological plates. I'm also into computer elements. And relaxants. I'm into shared ownership plans. I'm into—very big—cassettes. Recreation rubber. But you can't get fixed. No parameters. That's death. You can't define yourself. I mean, if I can't wake up on a Thursday, answer a call, and be ready for something called Cosmetic Truth, then I'm done. It's fine reception. And knowing when to close down. Sometimes you wipe out an entire region just because you sense—you *hear* it through the receiver while you're watching some guy trying to drink a Bloody Mary on his air mattress—you hear the breath catch and you know: That's it: the Middle Atlantic! Some other time, you rediscover a state. Last Tuesday I found Indiana! It was gone. No one was seeing it. The call comes. I get paged. I pick it up. The guy says, "Duplication circuitry," and there's Indiana! You have to be alert.

I take four other locals and nine long distances before lunch and bat about .458. It's a good morning. I dress. The lion is in the lobby on his four-foot tether and rug. He pisses on the sign: HAVE YOUR PHOTO SHOT WITH THE MGM LION. Actually, he's no relation. They cuff him. He smells like flat beer and blood. I drive downtown. I'm watching my weight, so I have a cold raw fish salad at the Nugget. "Hetchgar, the Kodiak Bear!" someone jokes. A lot of people I know move in and out. We exchange. I watch television. It's at the bar and Johnny Bench is slamming a triple under pressure against Philadelphia, so I store that. I watch five minutes of news. A guy in the bar says, "Too much government!" I say, "Not enough."

I check the pawnshops. I pick up an opal ring and go to Christensen's and have it appraised. It makes. I pocket it. My parents never lived to come here to this Electric City. They had a boating mishap off the Rhode Island coast. The harbor police found their sunglasses and thermos. My father loved birds. I buy some breath freshener and a copy of *Business Week*. I have my nails done. There's music playing in the room and I think about Korea in 1950; I hear artillery fire in the music and the manicurist, Trish, has my hand and is working on it and it's as if she's picked it out of the mud. More and more I see myself piecemeal. It's all addition. When I'm not here I'm in L.A. or Houston or Jersey City, but it's another man. Oh, the man it *is* is divorced too—but he's got no past. That's the difference. I tip Trish. She says, "Hey, thanks, Lee," and kisses me. I almost give her the ring.

In the afternoon, the pool is almost all Kansas City and Baltimore, soil nutrients and architectural forms. Kansas City's cocky. It ticks me off. I take a Valium between calls. I meet a girl from upper Michigan who's at a magazine distributors' convention, and she invites me to a party in the Molly Brown Suite after five. I accept. A rumor buzzes the pool that the lion's broken his chain, that he's torn open a lady's arm. People scream. I feel better. I deal with Kansas City. I say: "Fly out. I'll comp you at the MGM. You can have your picture taken with the lion. We'll talk." The voice gets hesitant: "What's the matter with dealing over the phone?" I tell them: "I have a special feeling about this negotiation." They go lower. I say: "It's not just price. Spend some time!" They underbid. I accept. The voice changes register. It goes on about chains they've just set up in Puerto Rico. I'm watching dives. I'm thinking—*way* back: of teaching swimming in Maine two summers, at a camp. There's an image: eight at night; boats and canoes moored and stacked around the T-dock; water like glass; air, cool as fish; my feet on rocks. The lifeguards are stacking chaises now. I see grass: lime wedges and swizzle sticks all around. Sunlight on garbage. People are clearing out.—One night in Maine I sat alone, not even wearing pajama bottoms, folded into myself all night long in a kayak in the very middle

of the lake. It was something else. There were stars. I thank
Kansas City for their cooperation. That's enough.

At the party there are complimentary soft-core and confes-
sion magazines everywhere. Paperbacks. People are auto-
graphing. Names are swooping out of pens like birds. I drink
my usual crushed ice and tonic. Sally Ann, the girl from upper Michigan, asks me what I think and I apologize; I tell her
I've never handled print. I confess: "Sally Ann, sweetheart,
I've never read a paperback book." A lot of people hear. They
listen. If you're not careful, listening can eat you up alive.
"Do you have a favorite author?" Sally Ann asks. "Right!" I
say: "One." It's for the listeners just as it's for Sally Ann. When
you're on . . . perform. But I *mean* it. "Who?" she asks. Off in
a corner I hear someone talking about the lion: "They trapped
him at the ice cream shop in the arcade and shot him." "Poor
son of a bitch!" someone else says. My favorite author comes
from my father's set of leather-bound books that he left. He's
the only author that I ever read. I mean always. William Blake!
"He wrote a lot about Las Vegas," I tell Sally Ann. She says
she's heard of him: "He's supposed to be interesting." I quote
from "I Saw a Chapel All of Gold." "This guy did *everything*,"
I tell her. "Wrote, drew." I don't like this group.

I take Sally Ann to the Bacchanal at Caesars for dinner. I
feel very sad. I feel like I would rather be water skiing. Water
makes this world. But that's not right. I *like* Sally Ann. She's
compact. She's enthusiastic. We talk about Mackinac Island
on the Canadian border and the fort there and the Grand
Hotel and the horse carriages and the bicycles and the banks
of flowers and ferry and finally the bridge. She keeps repeating two words that get *to* me: "another time." "It's all so from
another time," she says. She talks about John Jacob Astor. She
knows her Michigan history. She talks Indians. She talks furs.
Negotiation is in the sky again, and I feel at home. "So el-
egant," she says, "and from another time." A guy at the next

table is trying to tell the thinnest woman I have ever seen about what he's painting: "What I want to do," he says, "is an *Adoration*." He looks lost. I can only see his head. He looks like he's there, but he's in a snowstorm. People vanish. Where? And even the thinnest woman's lost him; she isn't listening. She's going on, her voice coming through a CB radio in her mouth, about "interstellar," and "transplanetary," and "them" and "voices." I start reading memos into my antipasto.

I start the wine. That's bad. I only ordered it for Sally Ann. I never drink, not hard stuff; that's not a problem; but, periodically, there's the wine. "You must have millions," Sally Ann says. I ask her if she heard about the lion. She says: "Poor pussycat." She has her hand on mine. I pour another glass. I think about the way light refracts through liquid. Water's powerful. It's a magnet for light. I think it must be interesting working with colors. I wish I had my copies of William Blake. I'd go right for the poem that begins: "The sun descending in the west. The evening star does shine . . ." Sally Ann asks me to teach her craps.

A guy in a black and white shirt with stills of Chaplin printed on it is rolling. I've never seen him. I have more wine. Sally Ann is asking me about the Field and about Big 6/Big 8, and I'm telling her: Negative. I'm explaining free odds. She has my elbow in her hands, both of them, tight, like it's a mast and she's holding on to it and we're in the wind. The Chaplin shirt is still rolling. I wonder what was the lion's name? Did he have a name? He must have had one; what was it? He wasn't just the MGM lion. . . . REX! I drink. My mind shouts: *Rex!* It turns to: *Wrecks!* The sloop that Sally Ann holds the mast of—*me*—heels, ships water, gallons over the gunwales, and begins to drop. I see hands only at the table, hands over trays. Some start going under. Did you ever just let your body drop? I mean, down? Sink down on purpose? Through the water on a lake at night? I have a line at Caesars, so I sign for five hundred and I play.

"I love it!" Sally Ann shouts. We're making numbers. We're repeating 5s and 8s and 9s. It's easy. Playing's easy. I rub Sally's back. I hate my hands. "Do you like this little lady?" I say—it's to the people next to me—"Isn't she nice? Isn't she a lovely specimen? Isn't she right from the heart of the heartland?" They smile. One guy says, "Right." What *is* this talk? Who *am* I? "What do we want?" Sally Ann asks. "What do we want? What numbers?"

"Lee!"

I tell her 10, 6, 5, and 4.

"Leland Hetchgar!"

I don't believe it!

"Lee! Jesus Christ!"

I'm looking across thirty years! He's there! The summer that I taught swimming in Maine, this guy taught canoeing. Randy Samuels! We haven't seen each other *since*. And he recognizes me! Boom! There we are: looking across history in the Electric City inside the pit at Caesars, and it's unbelievable. "Five!" Sally Ann shrieks. "Five!" Then "Four!" Time's an ocean. Time's a frozen ocean—with everything gliding, still, in the ice. Our hands reach out. Our hands are touching. We've got hold. "How's your J-stroke?" I say. "How's your cross-chest carry?!" he remembers. "Lee! I'm making number!" Sally Ann says. "Beautiful." I can't see her. She's outside the gel. "Son of a gun!" I say to Randy. And he says, "Son of a gun!" "Excuse me a minute," I say to Sally Ann. She's rolling.

So Randy's here, he tells me—but he's going. He's on his way. His firm is sending him to a seminar at Lake Mead and he's late. He's got a digital watch. We're both standing by Cleopatra's barge. "Hey, remember the campfires?" Randy says. My mind goes crazy. I'm smelling pine and applewood. I'm seeing embers. Hearing waves. "Bag the seminar!" I tell him. "Bag it! Stay!" He says he can't; it's business. A guy comes by delivering ice, crushed ice, to the bar. We swap addresses. I feel like someone's pulled the plug in my private pool. I want to grab and stop Randy from going out into the parking lot, to his rented Civic. "I just dropped a hundred at the blackjack table," he says. I say: "It doesn't *matter*. Here!" I'm yanking money. "I just won over a thousand."

He's backing! Now it's over. And we're breaking up. It's all shifting into pieces. "What about coming *back*?" I say.

"I fly out from San Diego."

He's gone. The door is shut. I'm standing with my money clip in my hand. The slots have gone bananas. The water's purple under Cleopatra's barge. Where's that painter?! Where's the painter that I saw? I should *show* him this. It's an interesting color. If I were useful . . . I can't believe Randy Samuels *knew* me. Christ! I'm forty-seven.

Sally Ann's trays are filled with chips. She's happy. She's bobbing up and down, like a life raft, in place. She can't see herself. I can see. I tell her, "Love, I don't know the time— but I'm heading back." She looks upset. She says, "I have numbers covered." I say, "I'll wait." I walk over to the bar. What do I want? I don't want anything. "Stay if you'd like," I tell Sally Ann. "They're *your* chips," she says. I say, "You bet them—keep them." She says, "No—just wait." She's very young. I imagine her on the deck of a ferry. Some are *deck* people, others, cabin. Someone sevens out.

Outside, Caesars' fountains are high and pluming. They're pink. "God, they're beautiful!" Sally Ann says. She has my arm. The air has cooled. The palm leaves are sawtoothed against the electric lights and I hear birds. It's only traffic and people moving, but it sounds like cockatoos. My father bought an Audubon print once of a snowy egret. He hung it over his bed. They had blue and green wallpaper in their room and the ceiling was painted white. All the furniture was wood. "I shouldn't keep those chips," Sally Ann says. I tell her, "Please." She pulls me close and gives me a very soft kiss on the mouth. "You're incredibly kind." "I'm not anything," I say.

Sally Ann has her head on my shoulder. It makes me drift. I feel like a bell buoy in a harbor. Fog carries the world. We walk past the main MGM entrance and go in by the arcade and fronton. A man is shampooing the carpet in the ice cream shop, all alone. It's all dark. I wonder if he's using special detergent for the lion's blood. The rug and stage and roped-off area *all* have been dismantled. "No more lion," Sally Ann says. *National Velvet* is at the movie. But it's gotten out. I go and stand where I think the lion must have been. I'm an endangered species. Sally Ann is looking through the store window at furs.

In the elevator, she says: "I have nowhere, I mean, in particular, to go." I thank her. The elevator stops and opens; it waits; no one's there. It closes up. "I'm serious," Sally Ann says. I say, "I know." She says, "Maybe you need me." I say, "May-be." She says, "Well?" Again I thank her. She says, "I have needs too." I say, "What time is it?" She says, "I don't know." I feel this elevator heading toward the moon. "Can you feel any gravity?" I ask. She turns. The elevator stops. "Seventeen-twelve," she whispers. It's her floor. She backs away. Her face is cracking. It's like I've dropped it and it's run through with little lines. I try to think of something: "Twenty-two-oh-one," I manage. But the door cuts off the "one" and I'm rising.

On all the corridors on all the doors, there are stars. Under mine, someone's slipped a note: "While You Were Out / Boston called / Memory Systems." It's another day! Twenty-four hours. It never stops. Who *am* I? How did I *get* here? There's a toll-free number. Why am I *doing* this? I turn the water on from both taps and from the shower. I feel better. I see my old camp and waterfront friend Randy, teaching canoeing on Lake Mead for his seminar. *Rough* stuff—special one-man maneuvers: C-strokes, sculling, crossing over his bow. Indians on the shore chant William Blake. I'm pacing. Joey

Bishop is on the television and I realize I'm moving back and forth across my rug, turning on a dime. The phone rings. It's Sally Ann. She says two words: "You're cruel," then hangs up. I wing a pack of matches at the mirror. They light. They're not supposed to. I put them out with my shoe. Thirty minutes ago, I was *incredibly kind.*

I need to shout. I need to pull curtains down and break apart the room. I need to kill the television. I need to overturn furniture on the rug. I need to fill the bath up with mud. I need to shatter the wind. I need to bellow. I need to go down and run, screaming, into the pit: Tearing clothes. Spitting. Biting. Slashing at people's faces: players, dealers, stickmen—ripping flesh. I need to lie—with all the lights out in the casino, all the wiring limp and dangling from the walls—on the craps table all alone in the dark, no clothes on, licking my skin.

I ride back down. I need something. I'm hungry. I wander out by the pool. It's like a ballpark at night without a game, only the people are missing. It's unnatural. I walk around. Something in the air smells like disinfectant or aftershave. I stand beside one of the telephones. At night, without the sun, without the sherbet and drinks and all the oiled bodies and talk, it seems more like a sleeping piece of equipment, or like a toy. I pick it up. It doesn't hum or vibrate or do anything; there's no tone; it doesn't operate. I move and kneel beside the water. God, it's still. I put my hands in, *into* it, and lift it to my face. I drop my head. Below the flat and quiet surface are two bodies at the bottom. That's the way it looks—at the deep end, through the chlorine water; but when I lift my head and wipe away my vision, I discover: they are only tiles. Still, there are fish and birds and animals in this night. And here I am.

Inside, the chandeliers look like ice. All the games are lean. I get a B&B at the bar. I travel with it. I travel nowhere at all. Then, at one of the blackjack tables, I see the painter. He's all alone. The thinnest woman in the world isn't with him. He's pushing chips, one right after the other, to the dealer. He's losing. The dealer's on a streak. The painter looks my way. He hesitates. He smiles. We both nod. It's recognition. He seems to know who I am.

Eagle

It was July and it was ten years after the United States had set a man on the moon and it was Tuesday when Cleveland Stokes began a series of discoveries. Cleveland was twelve and curious. His mother, Pearl—before the pickup accident and her coma—had called him Cleveland Curiosity. "Always poking about," she'd said. And so it wasn't surprising that after Gary— who was not exactly anyone's father—had left the mobile home to start his shift at the casino, Cleveland, just looking through things, made his first discovery: *the pictures.*

The pictures weren't anything like where they all were living. There wasn't any desert, even though there certainly was sand. And yes, there were rocks, but they were very different kinds of rocks, not mountain rocks at all. And Cleveland could see weeds and brush of a sort—but it wasn't the sage, and it wasn't the juniper, and those little scrub things weren't at all like creosote brush. It was . . . the Ocean. It was the Sea. And those words, "Sea" and "Ocean," seemed like very big, very distant, very powerful words to Cleveland Stokes. Like the Moon—that they'd been talking about all the time, it seemed, on radio and television the last couple of days, because it was the Moon Walk Anniversary. Like the Moon, the Ocean, and the Sea all seemed something almost fantastic, huge, almost unimaginable.

But there it was! . . . in what he took to be his mother's photos. Cleveland had found them in a book under some sweaters in a small closet in the mobile home. Before the rollover and the coma, his mother had read all the time, mostly paperbacks that she then boxed and stored in the casino warehouse. "Someday I'm going to start a library in this crazy dry town—the Jackpot, Nevada, Public Library! The Pearl M. Stokes Memorial Library!" She played with words, with names. So most books she stored. But there were some she kept and carried with her, and the one that Cleveland discovered the pictures in was a hardbound book with the title *To Have and Have Not,* by a man named Hemingway. Once Cleve had heard his mother say that she had come west, come to this part of the country, to be near the writer, Hemingway. Anyway, that was the book that had the pictures.

If Cleveland's mother, Pearl, had been there and not forty-five miles away in the Twin Falls Hospital, he would have asked her who the man, standing in nearly every one of the photographs at the sea's edge and beside a boat, was. *Is it Grampa?* Cleveland expected the answer to be *Yes.* Though he had never met his grandfather, his mother had woven quite elaborate tales. She'd gone on, always saying that Grampa Mason—"Honey, he just wasn't any kind of average man"—had come and gone, in and out of her life, a wanderer. He had been a fisherman, built a boat, cargoed rum and whiskey, drowned at sea and been risen to life at least five or six times, even "owned a railroad for one day." There seemed no doubt—even though young Cleve couldn't ask—that the man with the bare chest, the man with the open shirt, the man with the thick sweater and the knitted cap, that man was Cleveland's Grandfather Mason.

And if that were true, then the small girl in two of the pictures—standing on the man's shoulders in one, sitting on a boat gunwale in another—would be Cleveland's mother, Pearl Mason Stokes. Cleveland believed he had confirmation in the eyes. And in the smile. And in the length of her fingers. Because Cleveland's mother played piano—"Blues Piano, honey, it's a long story." Cleveland thought the voice in his mind, the voice that he'd not heard in almost three weeks. "If you're telling people, always say 'Blues Piano' . . . never just 'piano.'"

So with the pictures in the pocket of his blue chambray shirt, Cleveland listened one more time to the sound montage that the radio had been playing for the last two days, a montage of the United States moon landing, then turned the radio off and left the mobile home, starting out on a morning hike that would lead to his second discovery—the eagle.

The place, here—on the blown and mounded border of Idaho and Nevada—was *like* the moon. Cleveland, walking along the bed of the Little Salmon Falls River into the hills, once again, in his mind, replayed his mother, Pearl. "Honey, if your Grandfather Mason were ever, miraculously, to come back from wherever it is he's gone to, back from whatever star, come back and call me, reach me on the telephone and ask, 'Pearl . . . Pearl, Daddy's Girl . . . where is it that you've gone?' I would say, 'Daddy, the moon. Your baby Pearl's gone to the moon and is playing Blues Piano there, in the town of Jackpot. Life—silver dollars and a golf course—ringed by chalk, by lava rock, by craters!'" At night sometimes, Cleveland would step outside and stand in the high, weedy grass of the trailer court; he'd look up, see the shadowed satellite in the sky, and wonder, briefly, what planet he was actually on—until the music drifted to him from the casino.

Cleveland walked upstream. He moved between cliffs of volcanic granite, his sneakers and lower Levi's heavy with the water, moved playing his game, the game no one had taught him—it had been in the wind: *looking for gold.* He would pick shining rocks up, inspect them, knock glinting edges from the cliffs. Trout would flash, sometimes between his legs. Cleve would pocket the best rocks and try to mark the shore where he'd found them in the event that what he'd found might become a mine. In the casino gift shop, he'd found a book on Nevada ghost towns, towns built around gold, and he memorized the names, stringing them in his mind like an enchanted chain—Aurora, Jarbridge, Goldfield . . . !

But today, even playing the game, having the sun strike a stone, bending for it, drawing it out of the silver water—even doing all those familiar things—the song of towns, the voice in his mind saying towns, wasn't there. Instead there were conversations with his mother.

"Do I have a father?"

"Everybody has a father, honey."

"Who is he?"

"A man."

"Who's Gary?"

"A man . . . who lives in our mobile home with us . . . for now."

"Gary calls it a trailer."

"No, honey. No. It's a mobile home."

Cleveland hoped that his mother would open her eyes. He hoped that she would not be in a coma anymore. And that she would talk. And that she would play Blues Piano. And talk about his Grandfather Mason. And compare Jackpot to the moon.

"Why is our name Stokes?"

"Don't you like it, honey?"

"It rhymes with Cokes . . . and jokes."

"And folks. Well, sweetie-pie . . . it was the name of the man who was your daddy."

"But my Grampa . . . he was Grampa Mason."

"That's true . . . Stokes and Mason, that's true, there's a difference."

"Someday, maybe, could I be Cleveland Mason?"

"Well . . . it's possible. It's possible, honey. Anything is possible."

Cleveland wanted his mother, Pearl, out of the Twin Falls Hospital and home.

The eagle was trying not to move. It was an incredible thing for an eagle to do, restrain itself—unnatural. It had backed into a cavity in the granite and lava rock ledge, its wings poised for the flight it must have known itself to be too spent to make. Still, its eyes flashed. And its head, penciled by the sun, shining through a hairline crack in the upper ledge under which it crouched, looked cracked and fissured with light. The bird took all of Cleveland's breath. It stunned him. He stopped and found himself held stiller than the bird that was quite possibly larger than his own twelve-year-old frame.

It was like the first moment of the World!

"Hey . . ." Cleveland broke it—the silence, but in no way his awe. "Hey, bird. . . . Hey, eagle . . . what do you say?"

A great silent hum vibrated through the eagle's feathers.

"Hey . . ." Cleveland leaned his body forward slightly. He heard the Little Salmon Falls River rippling over his calves.

The eagle watched young Cleveland Mason Stokes.

"God!" Cleveland said.

Why wasn't the eagle flying? It was an adult eagle, huge, mammoth, male, a Golden. And though they were certainly not an everyday vision, Cleveland *had* sighted them—a million miles it seemed into the sky, soaring, sailing, defying every ounce of gravity with a grace of lines and circles. Had he dived for fish? Was he injured? Cleveland was convinced that if he could ever bring a thing this wonderful to his mother, Pearl, to her bedside at the Twin Falls Hospital, she would open her eyes and play Blues Piano again.

Cleveland swallowed what felt like the entire landscape, dry. He began moving his left hand slowly, slowly toward his front Levi's pockets, where he had stuffed some beef jerky. The two sticks were there, and he drew one of them, smoothly and cautiously, out, then extended his hand. He felt his tongue slip between his lips. "Eagle . . . ?" he said, saying it with all his stored curiosity, a question.

The bird's eyes fixed on the offered, cured stick. Some instinct, basic as bone and nerve, fired a new creature alertness in him; Cleveland even sensed it. The eagle was hungry! But it was a strange, cautious hunger; someone older and wiser than Cleveland might have called it *double-edged.* The eagle wanted food, yet seemed hesitant, doubtful that anything he might eat would nourish him.

"Here . . . !" Cleveland said and gently tossed the jerky into the rocks where the bird crouched. "There . . . it's there in front of you. . . . Go on . . . eat it."

The bird, with more caution even than Cleve had used dipping into his pocket, craned its neck forward to inspect, never dropping the reflected image of the boy in the stream from some peripheral facet of its eyes. It prodded the jerky, shifted it where it lay in the volcanic dust and sand.

"Eat!"

In one abrupt and riveting motion, the eagle's head darted forward, its claw-beak hooked the food, lifted and pulled it back. The stick of beef folded over itself and then was gone.

Cleveland felt that he had spoken to the eagle; he had

formed a word, then seen the bird's response. It thrilled and scared him that between himself and this enormous thing of the air, this feathered being with feet like braided golden hemp, that between them there might be some kind of exchange, even union. Cleveland drew out another jerky stick, tossed it, instructed, "Eat!" The bird ate, and still another bolt of thrill and terror made surge. Cleveland took a step toward the bird, saw all of its feathers flare suddenly and stiffen; so he stopped. "I won't hurt you. I will never hurt you, eagle," Cleveland promised.

Twice more that Tuesday, Cleveland Mason Stokes trekked in along the Little Salmon Falls River to his unmoving eagle, bringing beef jerky. Twice more he asked the bird to eat, and twice more the bird obeyed his instructions. Cleveland wanted to bring the eagle to his mother! In town, he had asked Lillian at the Treasure House why an eagle "would just be staying somewhere."

"Why do any of us stay somewhere?" she said—and Cleveland felt that he had missed something.

"No, I mean . . . aren't eagles . . . aren't they supposed to . . . ?" But when he saw Lillian's eyes staring just past the wire rack of Doritos, he let it go.

Would the eagle be in its place the next day? That question drove Cleveland nearly crazy all the late afternoon and through the evening. In his mother's sad absence, the casino had assumed meal responsibility, and so, in the coffee shop, having dinner with Gary, Cleveland asked, "Gary . . . you ever seen an eagle?"

"What do you mean?" Gary asked him.

"I mean, have you ever seen an eagle?"

"Hell, sure, everybody has," Gary said.

"Close?"

"What do you mean?"

"How close?"

"Hell, *I* don't know. You'd have to measure the air!"

Gary went back to his turkey croquettes. Cleveland went back to his burger special, but he couldn't keep it all inside. "Gary, I need to know," he said. "Why wouldn't an eagle fly?"

"Why's a dog cross the highway? Why's a train blow its whistle in the night? Why the hell'd anybody ever send a rocket ship to the moon? God, you got more questions than a tourist! Look . . . kid . . . just eat your burger."

Cleveland felt his eyes sting and start to float. He looked down at his plate, picked up a French fry. Who'd let Gary come to live with them, anyway? Gary didn't even have a last name as far as Cleveland knew. He dropped the French fry and slid along the booth seat to leave the table.

"You going to the john?" Gary asked.

Cleveland didn't answer. He just started straight out of the coffee shop.

"Maybe if he was sick!" he heard Gary calling out behind him before the bell and coin sounds of the casino, that and all the smoke, swallowed everything up.

An eagle, sick? How would that happen? Dizzy, maybe; resting; trying out the land for a change: all those reasons seemed more possible to Cleveland than an eagle's being sick. What would his mother say if she were to open her eyes, swimming up out of her coma, to see her son at her bedside with an *eagle*?

"Why, honey, thank you! What a nice . . ." What a nice what? What would she call it? What would she say?

Cleveland dreamed of wings all night. Of feet. Of eyes. He dreamed the eagle taking them, taking him and his mother, Pearl, to the moon. And Cleveland dreamed they found the ocean there, the sea. He saw his mother playing Blues Piano at night, on the beach, by the light of . . . not a moon; they were on the moon; something else . . . a huge CASINO sign in the sky. And Grandfather Mason was there on the deck of his boat, drinking rum and whiskey. And Cleveland—Cleveland of course was there, throwing sticks, driftwood, enormous distances into the air; and the sticks would be retrieved by the eagle, *his* eagle; no, the eagle of *all of them*. It was a wonderful dream!

Wednesday, the eagle was waiting. Gary left for his shift at ten past seven, and at seven-twenty Cleveland was in the water, running against the current, upstream, his pockets stuffed with beef jerky, and yes, truly, it was a miracle—the eagle had held its ground.

"Hi . . ." Cleveland said. ". . . Hello. Good morning."

He threw a stick of the jerky to the eagle, and the eagle took it and ate it. Cleveland moved a step closer. This time, the bird seemed not to flinch, not to electrify its feathers in the same way it had before. Cleveland fed the bird again.

"Why are you here?" Cleveland asked.

The bird looked at him, and some part of Cleveland, some private and religious part, fully thought the bird would answer. He quieted, grew reverent, waited. Had the bird said something? Had he missed it? Had his eagle responded?

Cleveland fed and fed the bird, stepping closer each successive time. By the seventh beefstick, the two were standing frame to frame, vision to vision, and the bird plucked the beef straight from Cleveland's hand. "Lord Almighty!" Cleveland said. It was an expression, words escaped from wonder, that he had heard from his mother. Incredible! He was feeding an eagle! He had an eagle eating out of his hand!

"Would . . . ?" Cleveland Mason Stokes tried like he had never tried in his life to form his words carefully. "Would you come? . . . to the hospital? . . . with me?" he asked. "For my mother?"

Cleveland's eyes widened to the size of planets. The bird was nodding! *Lord Almighty.* He swore the bird was nodding!

Then the eagle sent a hum, a kind of buzz-vibration down along the quill network of his feathers. The boy believed he had an answer.

He took his last stick of beef, stepped back half a dozen paces with it and held it out for the bird. They stood off, eye to eye, being to being, for a moment or so, and then—*Lord Almighty!*—the eagle started. He left the rock cavity and moved, with his ropelike and muscled feet, along the crushed volcanic earth until he arrived at Cleveland's shaking and outstretched hand and, once again, took the jerky.

Cleveland breathed. He exhaled nearly the entire sky before, checking his pockets and finding no more food for his eagle, he said, "Wait here. Eagle, wait here. I'll be back. I'll be right back with some more food." He eased away, making a quiet chant of his promise, always facing the eagle but moving downstream. He stumbled over a rock, left his feet, felt the chill Little Salmon Falls River rushing suddenly over him, righted himself, rose and began again, gently: "Just wait. We'll go to the hospital. I'll bring more food."

Stick by stick, length by length, journey by trip, Cleveland Stokes fed and coaxed the eagle downstream. It took three days. It took selling his skateboard to Raul Cortez, son of the head slot mechanic. "Cleveland—you are eating one hell of a lot of beef jerky!" Mr. Little of Little's Grocery said. "I don't know how you *consume* all this stuff!" Cleveland tried silence. But Mr. Little pressed. "How?" Cleveland's mother, Pearl, had said to him—*she seemed so close . . . and so distant*—"One thing I learned from the writer, Hemingway, was Be Honest. So, honey, if you can . . ." And then she always added, "I learned a few other things too. But I guess we won't mention those." So, when pressed about his quantity of jerky, Cleveland said to Mr. Little, "I have an eagle."

"You mean one a those sad dogs with the big ears?" Mr. Little asked.

Cleveland smiled, nodded, picked up his change, picked up his sticks of beef in their bag from the counter, thanked Mr. Little, and left. He had an idea burning in him, a chance, a possibility: bring Goldie—the name had *come*, just *come*!—bring Goldie to the midnight of his mother's mind. Goldie would carry her! Goldie would bring her across the sea. His wings! His wings would remind her of some constellation. "Honey, he's marvelous! Thank you for bringing . . ."

When they were close enough to be reached by the sounds of the highway, the interstate, the bird balked. He found some low, filmy-cool tamarisk and settled under it—poised, alert, stronger now because of the feedings, but reluctant. "Goldie . . . Goldie, come on," Cleveland tried again and again. But the eagle, clearly, had decided. So Cleveland settled into the nest with his friend, the enormous and quietly powerful bird, and he *talked*. "I wasn't there," he explained. "I wasn't with her. She'd gone over to Reno to get a saxophone and set of drums for the group at the Horseshu. And she had gotten them. And she was coming back. And I guess . . . I guess she fell asleep at the wheel. That's what Mr. Houston said." The eagle cocked its head; Cleveland was sure it was listening. "Did I tell you about my dream?" he asked the eagle and then proceeded to tell it all.

Later, around dusk, the two sat in the cool stream canyon together, in deep shadow, and just listened to the wind. "Do you believe in God?" Cleveland finally asked. "Do you think there are other worlds? . . . In the sky somewhere?" He left pauses in which perhaps in some way he believed the bird to answer. "Is water magic? Is fire? Are the rocks? The trees?" Finally, in the full dark, with only the rushing always of Little Salmon Falls River in the night, Cleveland stroked the bird's stiff, powerful feathers—it had come to that. "See you tomorrow," Cleveland said. "Get some sleep."

On Friday—the day before Goldie came to town—Cleveland brought a transistor radio out to the hidden nest. "What do you do with an animal who isn't doing just quite what you want it to?" he'd asked Gary at breakfast.

"Music," Gary had said. "Animals dig music."

"That's Waylon Jennings," Cleveland instructed the bird. "You like that song? That's Kenny Rogers. Come on. We've got the Rusty Clark Family playing in the Gala Room at Cactus Pete's 'til Sunday. You'll like them. Come on to town!"

He urged and urged. He tried food coaxing again. He tried putting his arm gently around the bird and making promises. "I'll get you some lamb chops. . . . You can have my bed, and I'll sleep on the floor." But the eagle had some sort of signal in its mind and wouldn't move. So Cleveland just sat talking for the rest of the morning and playing the radio: "You hear that? You hear that voice just then?" The stations were playing the Moon Walk montage still, periodically. "That was President Kennedy." And Cleveland tried to make his voice like the dead president's: *"We choose to go to the moon . . . "*

He needed help. And it didn't make the dream any less to be helped; Cleveland understood. Help from a proper person was okay.

In a way, it was surprising that he hadn't thought of Mr. Tigh before. Kenneth Tigh had come to America from Europe, from a country Cleveland always had trouble remembering the name of . . . Lithuania! And he had worked in New Jersey, northern Minnesota, New Mexico, and now here in Jackpot. He was auxiliary just-about-everything, security, maintenance, fire. He had taught Cleveland soccer—in the grass just above the new motel unit's clover-shaped swimming pool. And Cleveland knew he loved animals! Often, early in the morning, you would see Mr. Tigh on the seventh fairway of the golf course with his two Labradors and his one spider monkey, playing. So Cleveland told Kenneth Tigh the whole story of his eagle.

"He can stay in the fire station," Kenneth Tigh said. "All we have is half a truck."

"I'm going to take him," Cleveland said. "And he's going to get my momma out of her coma."

"I sure hope so." Kenneth Tigh put his hand down on Cleveland's head, as if he were going to do more than just rest it there—but that's all he did. "I think . . . I believe a boy should have his mother."

That evening, then, the two of them, Cleveland and Kenneth Tigh, brought the eagle the final distance. They took a tarpaulin and coaxed the eagle to the center of it with a cube steak. They'd roped the corners of the tarp in such a way that when Mr. Tigh, who was on a cliff just above the spot, pulled, the whole thing folded up like an enormous bag.

"He's gonna be mad," Cleveland had said.

And the eagle was. From the inside of the tarp came a sad, almost chilling shriek. It hurt Cleveland to hear it. It hurt him to think they'd tricked the bird, Goldie, who had become his friend. But after Mr. Tigh had backed his camper van down the riverbed, after they'd loaded the eagle in and driven back into town and brought him, sacked, inside the firehouse, after they had opened the tarp and freed the bird and given him two more cube steaks—the eagle seemed more than ready to forgive.

"You know what I think?" Kenneth Tigh was studying the eagle, observing stance and movement. "I would guess that what happened to this bird is that he got ahold of some coyote bait. Something's poisoned him. He's lost weight."

"Do you think maybe we could walk him over?" Cleveland asked. "To the casino? And just stand outside? And listen to the ten-thirty stage show? I promised him I'd do that sometime—and he really likes music."

Kenneth Tigh discouraged the outing. "Food and exercise," he said. "This eagle, I believe, needs good food and exercise.

Be two or three days before we can take him over to the casino."

So the two vowed secrecy. They would walk the eagle in the morning—the inside perimeter of the small gray cinder-block fire station, where the bird would leave its huge tracks on the earthen floor. Then Kenneth Tigh would hurry off to work. Cleveland would stay and play music for the bird, sometimes news. Kenneth Tigh borrowed an old black-and-white Magnavox that had once been in the employees' lounge, but the eagle didn't seem to care very much for television. He watched *Good Morning America* once when Reggie Jackson was being interviewed, but other times he'd just turn and meander anywhere away from the set. Noon hours, Cleveland and Kenneth Tigh took the camper pickup back into the foothills, and Mr. Tigh shot two, three, four rabbits—whatever he could find. Then the two would drive back and feed a rabbit to Goldie. Cleveland taught his eagle a sort of disco dance, a strange twisting double step that he and the bird would do together. But mostly they just talked.

"When my mother . . . after we go and get her out of her coma . . . then I think, maybe, that we'll go and live by the ocean," Cleveland said. "Do you like boats?" he asked. His eagle blinked. "I like boats." The twelve-year-old made it a statement. "I think boats are better than casinos."

"What would you like to be?" he asked the bird. "If you had a job, what do you think's a good one?" Cleveland imagined the bird's answering; he imagined the bird saying that he was perfectly happy being an eagle. "I'm . . . " Cleveland thought about it. "I'm probably going to be either . . . a sailor . . . or a writer—like Hemingway—or maybe an astronaut." The eagle moved across the dirt floor of the fire station—slowly, quietly—toward what he thought might be a mouse in the corner.

Cleveland kept pressing Kenneth Tigh about the hospital, wanting to take Goldie there to his mother. And Kenneth Tigh, gently, kept putting Cleveland off. But when it was no longer kind nor possible, Mr. Tigh agreed. "No promises. But we'll give 'er a try." So on the following Wednesday, they got Goldie in the back of the camper van with a live rabbit and headed off for Twin Falls. As they drove past the Horseshu Club parking lot, Cleveland saw Gary, his white dealer's shirt looking like electric milk, standing under the casino sign on a break, having a smoke. Something in the image—he thought he should wave, but his arm wouldn't move to do it—something in the image made Cleveland Mason Stokes shiver.

There was no moon visible in the Idaho sky. "Where's the moon?" Cleveland asked.

"It's obscured" is the way Kenneth Tigh put it.

Cleveland thought he knew what Mr. Tigh meant. But he wasn't sure. They drove in silence, listening to the eagle catch and eat the rabbit behind them in the van.

"You all right back there?" Cleveland rapped on the thin strip of a panel window that connected to the camper shell. The eagle didn't really answer. All Cleveland saw was a pretty large shape of feathers in the inside dark.

"We should have a plan," Kenneth Tigh finally said to him. "We should have a course of action for getting this eagle up to your mother's fourth floor, C-wing, semiprivate room."

"What about the elevator?" Cleveland said.

"More than that. More than that—we're going to need a lot more of a plan than that."

Cleveland could see sweat beaded on Kenneth Tigh's forehead. "Well," Cleveland said, "what do you think?"

"I don't know," Kenneth Tigh said. "I wish to hell I did."

"Maybe he could fly up to her window," Cleveland suggested. "Once we got there we could signal him."

"I don't know," Kenneth Tigh repeated. "I think maybe this eagle . . . I think maybe there's a fair chance he's forgotten how to fly."

"He can fly!" Cleveland thought the idea outrageous. If the

eagle had been only walking for the last week—well, then that was true only because it was the eagle's *choice*. He could fly. He could fly to the moon! He could fly anytime he wanted to!

"I had one idea," Kenneth Tigh said. "They tell you: use your resources, and I was trying to do that—use my resources—but I think actually what I came up with is . . . perhaps impractical."

"What is it?" Cleveland asked.

"Well . . ." Kenneth Tigh looked at his young friend. *Any* idea was better than mindlessness; any attempt better than resignation. ". . . If I go inside," Kenneth Tigh went on, "and borrow . . . do you know those carts? Do you know those carts like they use at the motel to throw the bedsheets in?"

"Yes . . . ?" Cleveland said in the moving camper, knowing that the rest of Kenneth Tigh's idea was still arriving.

"Well my idea is that—what if I go inside the hospital when we get there and borrow one of those? Carts. Then we can hide Goldie in it, under some sheets, and that way get him on the elevator, bring him up?"

"Good," Cleveland said.

Kenneth Tigh nodded. "Okay," he said. "I'll do that. When we get there. Get a cart. While you keep Goldie calm."

"Good," Cleveland repeated.

And Kenneth Tigh hoped, if nothing else, that he might help the boy to believe—absurd, yes, as it sometimes was—in *trying*.

They crossed the Snake River just at nine and pulled into the Twin Falls Hospital parking lot ten minutes later. The eagle was still and silent in the camper van, and when they slid the latch and opened the rear door, they could see him hunched, seemingly asleep, as if on a nest. "Goldie—we're here!" Cleveland called softly in toward his bird in a voice of undisturbed wonder and love. "This is it. The hospital! We're going to get her out from her coma!"

Kenneth Tigh switched on a Coleman battery light, its beam bounding off the dull aluminum walls, fleshing out the eagle, who appeared almost to be meditating. The bird *was* breathing, really: stately, compelling.

"Here we are, Goldie!" Cleveland urged gently, as his friend, the man, watched. "Here we go."

The enormous bird didn't resist or object. He felt ultimate trust for both the man and the boy. At the other end of whatever games they might play was, he knew, a rabbit, and the bird had learned to be extraordinarily patient.

"That's it." Cleveland spoke to his eagle. "That's it, girl . . . boy." And the bird emerged. The bird came forward.

The three—man, boy, eagle—rested a moment in silence at the back of the van, its gate down, looking at the window lights of the rising hospital. "Well, let's see what's possible and what's impossible," Kenneth Tigh finally said. Cleveland smiled. "You keep Goldie calm. I'll find a laundry cart." And Kenneth Tigh put his hand on the small boy's head, a gesture like the touching of a seashell or stone—awed, tender—then he moved away.

"We're going to do it, Goldie!" Cleveland promised the bird, and in his mind his voice had the precise sound of his mother's, once assuring. "Honey—someday, you and I, we'll go—get on a huge and silver airplane, and we'll just fly. We'll fly, we can do that!" *We choose to go to the moon . . .* He heard himself mouthing the dead president's words, so many times, recently, on the radio. And Cleveland found himself crying, his arms around the quiet eagle, torn with sobs. How Cleveland loved! How he loved and wanted his mother, Pearl, back! And he wanted Gary *out*, out of the mobile home. And he wanted to have the last name of Mason. Wanted! Cleveland longed for what he found extraordinary and far away—Mother, Ocean, Moon! He wanted these things almost unbearably. "Come on, Goldie," he said to the bird. "We've *got* to do it. I'll just tell them I'm bringing an eagle to my mother. I can't wait for Mr.

Tigh. Come on—attaboy." And Cleveland took a beefstick from his shirt pocket to coax the bird.

It was an awful helplessness that Kenneth Tigh felt when he saw that he'd startled the closer-than-expected eagle with his borrowed laundry cart—an awful helplessness. All he could do was watch.

He watched the eagle, which had been following Cleveland across the lot, begin, slowly at first and then with clear purpose, to extend its instinctive architecture: its feathers, wings. ("*No!*" he heard Cleveland shout.) He watched the shape fill with power, its pace accelerate. ("*No, Goldie!*") He watched the awesome bird's aeronautics as it hummed, lifted, spun, wheeling, massive up into the Idaho dark.

"*NO!*" Cleveland screamed. "Come back! Come down! Come upstairs with me, Goldie!"

But the moonless dark devoured the endangered bird. And the fireman friend of the boy felt as though it were his own heart being swallowed by a pitch-black, unflickering, fathomless sea.

"*Please, Goldie!!*"

Kenneth Tigh moved and held the boy in his arms and let him cry. Then, together, they rode the elevator up to Cleveland's mother's fourth-floor room. The room had only one dim, red-globed lamp, high, centered on a wall. His mother's bed stretched beside the uncurtained window; her eyes were shut; she looked thin. Cleveland studied her. Her skin looked white—very—and Cleveland could see some of its veins. Above the bed were suspended bottles with clear, strawlike tubes that traveled down, held by adhesive to his mother's wrists. "It's Cleve," he whispered. "Momma?" He said it several times, Kenneth Tigh's hand softly on the boy's shoulder the entire period. Dreaming in such a place seemed almost infinitely hopeless.

But then, sometime before the calendar change at mid-night, Pearl's eyes began to beat, slightly, behind her lids. And her lids rose up. And there was a kind of whir outside the just-barely-open hospital window. And she said a word—Cleveland's amazed eyes fastened to her, his heart flying—she said, "Eagle."

The Whorehouse Picnic

Chase watched Dixie cleaning herself over the blue plastic dish basin, sponging and laughing. The brain Chase liked, his *smart* brain, had thought something funny for Dixie, and Chase had said it, and Dixie had laughed, her stomach muscles tightening and relaxing. She was wonderful, beautiful, and Chase felt so good that he wanted to say his secret out loud, tell her about the bomb, describe how he'd heard a man on *Good Morning America* announce that any bright person could learn to build one by going to a public library, and that the man in the green suit and the bow tie had been right. Part of Chase, even at forty-one, in fact *was* bright. He had gone and read and found out and had been building an atomic bomb now for nearly seven years and was almost ready to test it way back in the Schell Creeks. Still, in his reading, once, on a trip to Carson, Chase had learned about the Rosenbergs and about their disclosure and where it had gotten them. But, God, she was beautiful! And he certainly wished she didn't work at Carole's 93 Club Lounge & Brothel, where half the men from the Ruth Copper Pit came, men who, except for his friend Pomo, Chase would turn down if they answered an ad to be his brother.

"You're adorable!" Dixie said.

"You have beautiful skin," Chase told her. He walked over and turned the Wayne Newton tape down on her Walkman.

"My skin stinks," Dixie said and laughed. "It's too tight on my bones. And it's like wax."

"Get dressed and walk outside with me," Chase suggested.

"Delores will put a hole in my head!"

"I'll pay another half hour."

"She doesn't want us hanging around out front. She says it's cheap. She says it looks like we're soliciting."

"Sometime I'm going to ask you for a regular date."

"Promises, promises!"

"So walk out back," he said. "Just put your robe on and walk out back with me. I want to stand outside with you just a minute."

Dixie looked at Chase. She squeezed some gel from a tube onto her hands and ran her hands between her legs, then over her breasts. "I'll say one thing for you," she said. "You're different."

"Good," Chase said. "I hope. I sure don't like most of what passes itself off for Life in this state."

"You don't like Nevada?"

"Nevada killed my mother."

Dixie took her robe off a brass hook. She knew what Chase meant; she'd heard his story—about how his mother's bones had changed to Cream o' Wheat before he'd even turned twenty and how it had happened to other people at about the same time, in the 1950s, in Caliente.

"Walk out back."

The dark outside was turquoise, veined and growing into new light. "This is what I like," Chase said, and he pulled Dixie in her orange silk robe to him like a colt or a calf. "I hate the mine. I hate the drunks. I hate the Fords and Chevies banked all along Steptoe Creek. And the Mustang Club. And the hotel. All the dealers who think *they're* beating you. . . . But I *do* like this. I like this air. I like this sky. And I like feeling my nose in your hair like this."

"You're a very different kind of person," Dixie said, her words against Chase's shoulder.

"You keep saying that."

"Well, it's true. I think you're probably very intelligent. Not that I think it's wrong to be intelligent. But things roll over in your head, like stones in a creek. And . . . *I* don't know: I get a chill, sometimes, when I'm listening to you."

"When's your next day off?" Chase asked.

"Monday."

"I'm going with Pomo . . . on a fishing trip, tomorrow, for three days. Up over into the Ruby Marshes. But we'll be back. I'm asking you to go on a regular date with me next Monday. Evening. No money. What would you say?"

"Where are we going?"

"I don't know. I'll have some trout. We could drive over to Ward Charcoal Ovens State Monument, and I'll grill them. And I could even bring us along some cold Blue Nun wine. We could start that way at least."

"Would you ever marry me?"

"Where'd that question come from?"

"What time?"

"About five o'clock."

"Okay."

Then Delores's voice sounded, "Dixie!" beyond. Dixie bit

Chase playfully on the neck and ran inside.

Driving his Silverado in the near dawn over to Hotel Nevada, Chase could almost smell the explosives in the back under his double tarpaulin. When Chase was a boy, the atomic bomb had started killing his mother. Sometimes he saw her ghost in the AG hosing down sugar beets and cucumbers. And it had made his father into a person who could rarely talk. Chase remembered the National Guard coming to Caliente and requesting vehicle owners to drive down to Earl's Sunoco for a free carwash. Chase had seen *Escape from Alcatraz* six times in his trailer on a VCR. "A person has got to free himself from what's bad," Chase had told Pomo, after the man had come seven years ago and talked on *Good Morning America*.

"I agree," Pomo had said.

"Then maybe he'll marry a woman who won't roll herself over in a pickup, drunk on Oly beer."

"Damn rights," Pomo had nodded. "Damn rights. You definitely got yourself a winner there—with that attitude."

Chase almost ran his van into the back of a '76 Camaro. He pumped his brakes. So if you were smart enough, then maybe you could stop hating your life. True: Chase's bomb wasn't *exactly* like the 1945 bomb. Still, according to what he'd been able to read, he had the essentials. So Chase probably wasn't a fool.

Waiting for his *huevos rancheros* in the Hotel Nevada coffee shop, he drew nuclei and neutrons and gamma rays on his napkin. His eggs came. The Mexican waitress asked, "You make a map?"

"*Sí*," Chase said. He cocked his head. He laughed. Then he said, "I'm sorry."

The Mexican waitress looked confused.

He called Pomo to set the time that they would leave for their fishing trip to the Ruby Marshes. His mind was still full of Dixie. Pomo said he was waiting. Chase said he needed the morning for other things. "What *other things*?" Pomo wanted to know. Chase said he would pick Pomo up at two.

"You have salmon eggs?" Chase asked.

"Three kinds," Pomo said. "And cheese marshmallows. And garlic cheese."

Everybody at the pit treated Pomo as an Indian. Chase knew he wasn't. Chase knew that when Pomo was just a little boy, he had lived in a palace in South America somewhere. He and Pomo had talked. Pomo had told Chase that one night many men had climbed up over the palace wall and Pomo's father had told Pomo that he should run and that he should never come back, and Pomo's father had shown Pomo a passageway underground and Pomo had run until the passageway had come up in the woods, in some trees. Then, over time, Pomo had ended up in Ely, Nevada. "I'm not an Indian," he had said to Chase. "I was a boy in a palace." Chase respected Pomo.

Chase hung up the phone and looked out over the lobby and the casino of the Hotel Nevada. Everything was dead light and dust. The carpet looked unraveled and like lint. The furniture was fat; it was tired and scarred. The whole thing was like a waiting room, Chase thought, for people who were so bored they had made appointments to die. One man, with a blue hard hat on, playing alone at a blackjack table, had a cup beside him, the coffee steam seeming to slide *down* and over the ratty felt and never to rise. It was a place you could never repair or renovate. All you could do is blow it up and start over.

Chase had built his bomb in the Schell Creek Range, in an abandoned shaft where a man named Hildebrand had once prospected for gold. Chase had found Hildebrand's claim in a can. Approaching, over the rutted road, always made his pulse beat in his head, afraid that some rock or sudden ditch would upend the van and set everything off. His brain made pictures of enormous craters and of huge funguslike clouds all along the unimproved thirty-seven miles.

He parked at the mouth of the shaft and put the tailgate down. The mine went back a hundred and thirty feet and averaged five feet in height. This was his last load, and Chase unwrapped it and packed it in and attached it up so that when he was done, his atomic bomb, radio-timer-detonator included, was in the side of Monitor Mountain and ready to test.

He'd rigged a pulley, and with it he packed a flattened '52 DeSoto against the shaft. Then he piled rocks. Sometimes he felt *outside* his bomb. Other times, he felt *in* it. It was curious. Also he felt very solitary with what he'd done. Was that how the fellow, the scientist, Edward Teller, the man he'd read about, had felt? And the other man? Oppenheimer?

But he also felt proud. He was not the stupid person that some tourist, seeing him leave the Ruth Copper Pit, day shift, black lunch pail in his hand, might think. All Chase needed now was to set his CB radio to the proper frequency at the proper time and the whole mountain should go off.

Chase imagined a conversation with Dixie. "It's an atomic bomb," he would say and point. "There. In the mountain."

"God! Amazing!"

"It took seven years."

"You have to be a genius!"

"I built what I hated," he would say, "so I could stop hating it."

He brushed his hands. He looked down. He looked at the dust. He looked at the mountainside and saw a mule deer bound into camouflage. He looked at the chill broken light, now at noon, through the trees. Red-tailed hawks nested here. His muscles felt hard. His brain had a fire. He would fish with Pomo, who'd grown up in a palace! He would land enormous trout! He would find a place somehow, somewhere, with Dixie.

Pomo was standing out in front of his shack when Chase arrived, practicing casting with a chicken bone at the end of his line, tied there with a nail knot.

"How're they biting?" Chase asked Pomo.

"I caught a small dog," Pomo said. "But I threw him back."

"Shove your gear in the back," Chase said. "Just unlatch it."

Pomo gathered a bedroll and backpack and tackle box with his rod and moved out of Chase's vision until he filled most of the rearview mirror, throwing up the hatch on the back of the vehicle.

"You ready for the big ones?" Chase asked his question to the mirror.

"What're you doing with *this*?" Pomo asked.

Chase could feel an oily jolt snake his spine. He set himself and turned slowly around, knowing that he would see what he saw: Pomo holding a stick of dynamite that had hidden itself in some fold of tarpaulin. "I smoke that," Chase said.

Pomo looked at the dynamite, then at Chase, then at the dynamite, then at Chase again. "You gonna blow lunkers out of some hole you scouted?" Pomo asked.

"Who knows?"

"You steal this from work?"

"One thing I have to tell you," Chase said. "We can't turn on the radio. It wears the battery down. It's important." Chase had not *planned* exactly when he would set the bomb off. Maybe he would just drive around for a year or so, knowing that he *could*. Or maybe he would set it off Monday night, on his regular date, and impress Dixie. Still, he tried, nevertheless, to make it clear, without hurting his friend's feelings, that the CB radio had to be out of bounds for Pomo. "I mean it," Chase emphasized. "Don't turn the radio on. I'm extremely serious."

They drove past the gravel pit through Ruth and over Little

Antelope Summit. At Eureka, they turned north on 46, up along the Diamonds, along Huntington Valley, then, just before Jiggs, east to Franklin Lake and the Ruby Valley Indian Reservation. They talked about the day. "I like the shape of the sky," Pomo said. Then they argued whether sky actually had *shape* or not. They ran down lists of people on the crews they worked with.

"You like McLaren?"

"If McLaren had a brain, he'd be dangerous. You know Luker?"

"Luker has to sleep with snakes. Angelari?"

"Angelari's a loser."

"Definite loser."

"The next time Angelari takes a bath, it'll be the first."

There were random thunderheads when they set up camp, and they could hear a far, offhand rumbling that neither took to be dangerous.

"Think it'll rain?" Pomo asked.

"I don't care if it does."

They walked the Franklin River along some railroad tracks. Neither had fished the area, but a man they'd met once on the Owyhee River had recommended it.

"There are trout in there." Chase pointed down to where a drape of reeds flagged along a section of the bank.

"How do you know?" Pomo asked.

Chase touched his glasses. "Polarized lenses," he said. "Cuts the surface glare. I can see them."

Pomo studied Chase. He nodded. "You've got brains," he said. "You are one guy with brains if I ever met one. You figure things."

Chase enjoyed Pomo's respect. It occurred to him to tell Pomo his secret. Instead, Chase asked whether Pomo had ever thought about marrying.

"Maybe you and I'll talk about it sometime," Pomo said. He picked a handful of gravel up from the rail bed and hurled it.

Chase resented Pomo's gesture. His privacy. Were they friends or weren't they? Did they discuss things or didn't they? Did Pomo think that just because he'd grown up in a palace he was better than Chase? Chase's impulse was to fish a hole off somewhere by himself for what was left of the afternoon.

They fished a wide bend together, just below where a fast, churning creek angled in from the north. There were eddies and holding pools and a lovely, smooth V just above some swifter ripples. Pomo landed a sixteen-inch cutthroat. Then Chase hooked an enormous brown. "Holy shit!" Chase said. The drag on his reel made a sound like Dixie sometimes made. The brown broke water. "Jesus Christ!"

"He's a monster!"

"You bet he's a monster!" Chase said. "That's a monster that's been in that pool for a *million years* just waiting for me!"

"Don't let him head over toward those logs!"

"I'm watching him!"

"He's headed over toward those logs!"

"Get out your net!"

"He's going to wrap himself around those logs!"

"Let *me* worry about that! Get your net out!"

"He's *in* there!"

The enormous brown tangled Chase's line around submerged tree roots; Chase lost the fish's resonance against the play of his fingers, the direct tension. He felt blood pumping into his face and scalp and arms and charged, working his reel, into the stream. "What are you doing?!" Pomo shouted, but Chase rushed the logs and his submerged trout. He fell, scrambled up, fell, scrambled up again. "Chase! Jesus! Be careful! Don't be crazy!"

He was not going to lose this! He had lost too many things here where hope just went up and blew back so hot and dry that your breath felt like ashes. He had not made a date with

Dixie or spent probably ten percent of his life building an atomic bomb for *nothing*. Chase dove into the pool.

Underwater, he searched for his trout. He grabbed a log, let his pole go but followed its filament into the hatchwork of branches. He felt strange. He felt in danger. He felt a delicious madness. Then Chase's hand touched skin, and he knew that the brown was still possible; and he almost shouted. He could feel his chest beating. He could feel his breath wrestling with itself, making itself still. Then the yellow belly of the brown flashed. Chase's better brain ordered his breathing to relax. He could see the root that the brown had wrapped himself, again and again, around. And with one hand to the right of the snarl, the other hand to the left, Chase positioned himself, feet planted in the rocks of the streambed, and twisted, rotating the root so that, somehow, it snapped just outside both his hands, and he rose to the air and to Pomo's vision of him with the branch high and level over his head and the enormous brown he had chased dangling from it. "*Bring the net!*" he yelled.

That night, Chase made a package for his trout with aluminum foil. He poured dark rum in and closed the package and buried it in the coals of their fire. He and Pomo sat on rocks and passed the rum bottle between them. "You should use lemon," Chase said. "And butter. But I didn't bring them." And then he confessed to Pomo, "I may love Dixie." Pomo nodded. He passed the rum bottle to Chase. They could hear an owl, in a nearby tree, eating a potgut.

Later, suddenly, Chase was awake, bolt upright in his bedroll and crying out. The earth lifted. The whole eastern sky trembled and flared. It was like being in the belly of a world suddenly enraged. He felt terrifying failure, awful loss. But he understood, too, in an instant, what the moment was all about. He knew. Pomo was sitting, door open, in his Silverado with the CB radio on, looking ashen. "Oh, fuck," Chase said. "Goddammit-shit-piss-crap-and-doublefuck!"

"Jesus Christ, man!" Pomo said. "What was *that*! Chase, man, *look*!" But Chase was already looking. "I couldn't sleep. I got up," Pomo said.

Well, there it was!

"I took your car keys from your jacket pocket and . . ."

Boom!

". . . figured if I couldn't sleep, then I'd get some company."

Seven years!

"And so I turned your CB radio on, and I was dialing back and forth, looking for a band, when . . . !" And all Pomo could do was gesture toward where the sky was green like phosphorous and making sounds like a huge, hungry stomach.

"I told you twice . . ." Chase contained himself. ". . . driving over here . . ."

He gritted his teeth. ". . . I said . . . I *warned* you . . ."

Pomo swallowed.

"*Don't use the radio.*"

Pomo wet his lips. "I forgot," he said.

Two mornings later, Chase and Pomo shoved their gear and their Coleman cooler full of trout into the back of the Silverado and started home. Pomo had been a rage of questions. Chase wouldn't talk. Something had been taken away. Something had been made incomplete. "But what could it have *been*?" Pomo kept asking. And "Chase—really—shouldn't we *leave*? Shouldn't we get a paper and *find out*? Maybe it was the *mine*. Maybe it was the *pit*. Maybe it was the whole of *Ely*. Maybe something happened."

They stopped for coffee in Eureka on their way home and bought a paper. The paper had a picture of an immense crater on the front page and the headline: ENTIRE MOUNTAIN COL-LAPSES EAST OF ELY. The article kept repeating phrases: "confounds scientists" and "baffles experts." And at several points it said things like "with the near force of a thermonuclear device." Chase felt some part start to shift position inside himself—though he wasn't sure, really, what it was.

"Aren't you *interested* in this?!" Pomo said.

"What's the deal?" Chase said. He thought of Dixie. He tried to stay remote. He tried to act dispirited and failed. "A mountain blows up. So what? I'm glad no one was injured. That's all. Or killed."

"*Look at this!*" Pomo pointed to a whole inside page of pictures of the crater. "Sure, they *say* no one died. But there are all kinds of people—sheepherders, prospectors—living up in those mountains. Twenty years from now! *Then* they'll start giving a list!"

Chase felt confused. He pushed his coffee mug away and stared into the gallon jar of beef jerky on the counter as if it would answer something.

He sat in his trailer most of Monday and thought of taking his life—it made sense—but he worried he would hurt Dixie's feelings if he didn't appear at five that afternoon for their first regular date. So he washed. And shaved. Put a clean shirt on and a string tie. And he drove to Carole's 93 Club Lounge & Brothel at the time he and Dixie had set.

The door was locked. The lights were out. Dixie came around the far corner of the building. "Hi," she said.

"Hi," Chase said.

She was wearing an orange summer dress with spaghetti straps. "I have some bad news," she said. "I'm sorry."

"What?"

"I should have remembered—but I'd forgotten."

"You don't have the day off?"

"No—it's the picnic."

"What do you mean?"

"It's the whorehouse picnic," Dixie said. "We have it each year. Did you hear about the mountain?"

"I did," Chase said. "I read about it in the paper. So you can't see me?"

"We have the picnic. It's at the natural arch. Up Elderberry Canyon. It's just us. Once a year. No one else is s'posed to be invited."

"You look beautiful," Chase said. And just then, an orange White Pine County School District bus pulled up in front of the brothel. "When is it through?" Chase asked. "When's it over?"

"It depends," Dixie said. And she came close and gave Chase a kiss on the side of his head.

"*It's here!*" Chase could hear Delores calling out to the other girls inside.

Chase couldn't help himself. He started home, but then drove up to Elderberry Canyon and parked in a turnout before the natural arch. He could hear shrieks and music, and he approached through trees to see all the women from the brothel arranged—plastic drink glasses in their hands, some with paper plates. Carole was grilling steaks on a standing fireplace. There was a large battery tape deck playing Bette Midler from *The Rose.* Dixie was there, talking with a girl named Satin and another girl Chase had never met. It was curious. It made Chase feel wonderful. It made him feel shy.

He stayed in the trees, circling, and the dusk came on. At one point, someone saw him and pointed and Dixie gave a tiny wave, but no one seemed really affected. When the dark came, Carole and Delores set halogen lamps around the picnic's circle, and the girls all started to dance. Someone put on a Neil Sedaka tape. Someone lit the lamps. A number of the girl couples close-danced; some even kissed each other with their mouths open. They were all high. Chase found himself with his arms wrapped around a lodgepole like a wife. His bomb only came to his mind once, flickering, like the wings of a bat. He watched Dixie. She danced with Annette. But it was friendly dancing. They joked and teased. Once they danced cheek to cheek.

Chase stayed on the edge, in the trees, watching, until midnight, when Delores called that the bus would be leaving in ten minutes. Then he came out and signaled Dixie. She strolled over. "You obliged to drive back with them?" Chase inquired.

"I'm off 'til noon," Dixie said.

He looked at her. It was hard to talk.

"I wouldn't mind driving over to see the Red Lion in Elko," she said. "I haven't seen it—and they say it's nice."

So they did that. Dixie threw up out the van window once, just north of Currie. She'd had too much to drink. She apologized. "They've surely done a good job with this," Dixie said when she saw the new Red Lion Casino and its impressive carpet. Chase bought her a breakfast steak in the coffee shop; then they took a room and undressed in the silence.

"It's different," Chase finally said.

"Yes, it is," Dixie said. She was standing near the light from the window. "It is really . . . So? Well? What would you like?"

"What would *you* like?" Chase said. "You always ask me. What would *you* like this time?"

She told him. And he tried. And it seemed to work. Just after four, they woke up a Justice of the Peace, behind the Commercial Hotel, and married each other and drove back to Ely with Dixie's head on Chase's shoulder, talking about different planets that were in the sky sometimes that you could see.

They were tired, and they went to sleep for a couple of hours in Chase's trailer. Chase scrambled eggs for them and made them toast and coffee for breakfast. They smiled at each other, then Dixie said: "Have to get to work." And she stood up and kissed Chase on the cheek, and he kissed her.

"You want to take the car?" he asked.

"Why don't you drive me?"

So Chase did. Then he went to the Hotel Nevada for a third cup of morning coffee. And sat. And looked around. And he had to admit—it had the look, somehow, of a different place.

Salvage

Like everyone else I have come to this place where no person was born, and like others, I am blindly hopeful. *Here it is!* I think. And I watch the others cast their eyes east, then west in a kind of pride, then disbelief. We have not known such air ever, air that stiffens and drives anything lubricated underground. And we have only known sky like this once, when it lay black and deep, under us, as water. And so it's right that, each one, together we populate this desert now to raise a ship.

I could list where I've lived. Orono, Maine. Lakeland, Florida. Belmont, Massachusetts. St. Paul, Minnesota. Paducah, Kentucky. Washington, Iowa. White Sands, New Mexico. Stanley, Idaho. McCall, Idaho. Twin Falls, Idaho. Jackpot, Nevada.

I'm a finish carpenter. Once I thought I would like to live in Orvieto, Italy.

But where any of us live doesn't matter, though, in such a venturing world made for the raising up of troves. Because we'll stop living where we live always and start paying visits to the liquor store. Boxing our books. Stacking plates, coffee mugs. We'll pack all of our towels, bedsheets, soaps, lotions, medications. We'll put shoes here, empty what we've used for a desk somewhere else. We'll flank television consoles using cardboard we've broken down, pillows. Hand-carry the vacuum. Fill our soft luggage with clothes. There are Ryder vans of all sizes.

Why I moved so much *within* and not *out of* the state of Idaho and for so long is that it's volcanic. There are lava fields north and south, purplish craters, hovering pumice shapes raised against the yellow-green of an alfalfa sky. Water spills out of blistered pocks high along mesa ridges, drops hundreds of feet into fish hatcheries. Something in the idea of a world once amniotic, *molten,* stopped me—caught me, held me—even briefly.

But "even briefly" is, of course, just that—briefly—because there's the need, I've learned, for finish carpentry everywhere. And so I left Stanley, Twin Falls, McCall—left Idaho, drove south, snaked my Cherokee up the full rise of Galena Summit. Past the River of No Return. Then descended. Followed Interstate 93. Down through Ketchum. Through Shoshone and Picabo. Rogerson, Jackpot, Contact—down through Wells. Nevada: Ely; down through Ash Springs and along the outskirts of Caliente.

And all the while I thought: *Is this what's happening? Is this the truth: the world, in fact, getting less conical and eruptive? myself winding down toward what could be a riverbed, a settlement?* Shapes appeared—figurations, formulations in the vastness. Birds, flying in and out of the rocks—larger and then diminishing, seeming to be not birds at all. But rags and ashes.

Then, at midnight, all the lights of Las Vegas electromagnified the sky, fifty miles away, and I set my course—no notion then, of course, of now. Here, being witness. If another person had said that weeks, *months* after my arrival, people would gather, see the desert be water, raise a ship—I would have shaken my head.

Where I am, then, has no existing map. It's west and north—but where? Where precisely? Because we are only where our events deliver us. We drift—slip past trees and toward rocks—inch forward, foot by mile. One doesn't simply wake, brew coffee, gather up one's lover in a black Cherokee, drive to the desert, salvage a ship. There are circumstances.

Water broadcasts; electricity whispers. Las Vegas is all mute-at-best disclosure. It's in the cars on Maryland Parkway; people whisper into cellular phones. Waiters whisper into the fish they serve at the Tillerman; clerks lean into each other at Neiman Marcus. I've seen women whisper into their quarter machines at the Lady Luck. And all the pit bosses breathe secrets to the floor managers. But I'm wandering.

It was two in the morning when I unpacked the last box in my Prince Albert Apartment off of Koval. I like not going to sleep. It stokes the chance that everything is continuous. So I wandered out, ventured the back lanes over to the Flamingo Hilton. It seemed pink. Dusky. Like a parts factory. So I crossed Las Vegas Boulevard over to Caesars, bought a *Journal,* sat in the kidney-shaped Café Roma and had miso soup, dry wheat toast. There were eighteen Help Wanted ads for finish carpenters. It was the middle of the night. The third ad I called, the man said, "Be at the Ponce de Leon Lakes complex at 6:30 A.M." So I was hired.

I had three hours to lose. I had never played dice; I played. A man, who was from Aruba, beside me, showed me how. I won twelve hundred dollars, had a plate of chicken livers, drove south, and found the Ponce de Leon Lakes. I started work.

It's been good work. Steady. Christensen Foundries and Construction. The company moves me. After Ponce de Leon, I went to Seven Cities of Gold—also south but toward the foothills. "Finish" is a relative term. In Las Vegas, if you step back from what you're doing to consider it, and what you're doing involves cabinets, you're a finish carpenter.

I made a friend. No, that's not exactly true. Charlie West. Charlie never talked, although he hummed often. He'd studied studio art at Indiana, then, for a while, played vibraphone; perhaps that's what accounted for the humming. But he lived near, just off Tropicana, and being proximate counts. So we carpooled.

Charlie worked with stone and imitation marble. Sometimes he made rocks for waterfalls. Sometimes I would borrow his buffer. Sometimes he'd need my linseed.

Also I met Lacey Ames. Lacey Ames dealt twenty-one at the Luxor. She was a surviving identical twin and believed in pyramids. I built a rosewood and Lucite one over her bed and suspended another—smaller, cast-aluminum with rice paper—over her kitchen table. She said the minute it was in place she lost weight.

So I worked. Carpooled with Charlie West. Began, I believe, to fall in love with Lacey Ames—if love folds and rumples like sheets. And I watched people—*every*where—slow and shift and list and lean into each other, telling secrets.

One secret, in my fourth month, had to do with the ship—*here*; this place; this gathering—and its salvage. Actually, at that time, in May, it had, more specifically, to do with the desert.

It was after work. Charlie West was driving; we were in his little Datsun, the pickup, except the direction was north. "Where are you going?" I asked.

At first Charlie didn't answer. He could hum Gershwin and make it sound like Bach. Then: "You need to see something," he said. His words—five, in a row—surprised me.

We drove west, then a little north, then west again. Every-thing, where it wasn't flat, was all cutrock and rabbitweed. Then Charlie turned north again onto an unimproved road that was barely surfaced.

"You want to talk about this?" I asked.

"I think not," he said.

We looped, wound, rose up. There were still maybe two hours of light. The air outside had exhausted itself, spent its heat and smelled like alcohol. There were juniper and Joshua scattered—berries and pods black against the light. Ahead I could see the scaffold for a core drill. And a red-bearded, redheaded guy—black jeans, blue T-shirt—standing by the core. He wore a straw pirate hat that said, TREASURE ISLAND.

Charlie parked. We got out. The red-bearded guy waved and we started toward him. "Hey! Hey, Charlie!" he said.

"Hey, Charlie, yourself," Charlie West said. They were both named Charlie. "Show him," Charlie West said.

"Charlie Baines," the other, the second Charlie, said. He held his hand out.

I introduced myself.

"Show him," Charlie West said again.

"We've got something," Charlie Baines said. "Happening. Happening here." And he walked us to the core drill.

Why he was there, he said . . . why they were sampling was this: Christensen's hoped to develop either Juniper Lake or Joshua Lake—I. Soon to be followed by either Juniper Lake or Joshua Lake II and III. It's what brochures call a Phased Living Complex. The Big Question was, the earth—the base, its composition, what they would build on—was it mineral-rich? How solid? Were there plates?

"Here's the culprit," Charlie Baines said. And he closed his hand over the core drill. Then he walked Charlie West and myself over to a rickety pine table, where he'd set out three lids of mason jars, a different sample in each one. He indicated the first. "This squib of planking is Norwegian pine," he said. "Down about two hundred feet."

Charlie West looked at me. It was that look that said, Isn't that amazing?! But I'd missed it, missed the amazing part with the Norwegian pine.

"It's not indigenous." Charlie Baines picked up on the discomfort and said, "It's never been indigenous. You go back Pliocene in this place, you don't get wood pulp like Norwegian pine."

"He's an archeo-zoologist," Charlie West whispered. The word "archeozoologist" made a *thrummbbb*, like a cicada.

I just nodded.

In the second mason jar lid were *different* fibers—gray, yellow—bristly.

"Sisal," Charlie Baines offered. "Rope. Hemp. Halyard."

"From . . . ? Where?" I asked.

"Same place," he said. "Down. Down there. Same as the pine."

"Underground?" I said.

Now Charlie West was smiling.

"Two hundred feet," Charlie Baines said.

"So . . . how does rope get underground?" I asked. "That far?"

Charlie Baines raised a cracked index finger in a gesture that said, You just wait! Wait a minute! Then he swung his body around so it was facing the third mason jar lid.

In the third were a couple of soft-metal curlicues. Colored gold. They looked shaped and augured by the half inch of the core drill.

Charlie West could barely keep his feet planted under him.

"What are those?" I asked.

"Pieces," Charlie Baines said.

"Of?" I asked.

"Gold," Charlie Baines said. "Coin, jewelry. You tell me."

I reached out and secured the lid. Brought it close. Charlie Baines relayed a magnifier, which I set over the gold. The fragments. On one, I could almost see lettering, glyphs, lines—some angled parallel, others looping.

"Same place?" I asked.

"Same place," Charlie Baines said, his voice proud.

"So what do you think?" Charlie West asked.

"So then—are you saying . . . ?" I began.

"Absolutely!" Charlie Baines said.

"That there's a *ship* down there?" I said. "Sunken? A treasure ship? One with gold?"

"Absolutely!" Charlie Baines said again.

Norwegian pine, sisal, lettered gold: it seemed possible.

Everything was once its opposite. I've learned that. Fire, at one time, was air. Water was fire. Earth was sea. So it's, of course, not unimaginable that at some distant point, tall ships transported wealth from one civilization to the shores of another. And that they did it across where, now, sand blows, where bristly juniper and strange, lopsided Joshua trees flower. *Once upon a time,* as the story goes. *Once upon a time, in this place, there sailed a people . . .* And so on. So forth.

Just like that, then, I'd been confederated into a secret. Because a car drove one place and not another. Because—who knows?—too much sky hovers over some forsaken ground. A man goes on a job. *Test the earth.* He does. It's routine; drill and sample. Then, more than two hundred feet under the desert, he finds a ship. What next? It seemed a question larger than the imaginations of two people.

"You know, we could be famous," Charlie West said.

"Or even more. *Next* thing," Charlie Baines said.

"What are the trove laws?" I asked. I'd learned a little about trove laws when I'd worked in Florida.

"None," Charlie Baines said. "Nevada *has* no trove laws. It's all open. It's all up for grabs—I checked."

Charlie West watched for my reaction; I seemed cast by him in a specific role.

"So who knows? Who else knows?" I said.

"No one," Charlie West said.

"Then, *theoretically,* you could write up a . . . say, report, citing land as . . . problematic. Above some . . . *fault* or something," I suggested.

The two Charlies looked at one another. Charlie Baines pulled open the drawer of the pine table. He pulled a document out. Held it up. Smiled.

"I see," I said. "I see."

They waited.

"Okay—so who owns the land?" I asked.

"The Forest Service," Charlie Baines said.

"But they'll sell," Charlie West said. "Christensen just has short-term. Their lease."

"But . . . okay; but okay, sure: you dummy a report, buy the land, bring a treasure up—Christensen'll come at you with a hundred lawyers . . . take it away."

"That's right," Charlie Baines said.

Charlie West nodded.

"Still, I'll tell you now: there's a lot of gold down there," Charlie Baines said. "I've been bringing up coins. Coins and coins. Coins and coins and coins. Everywhere I punch, almost. *A lot* of gold. I'm talking *lot.*"

"I . . . let me think about it," I said.

Charlie West seemed disappointed. He cracked the brim of his Oly cap, cracked it up, then down again. He had expected some kind of diagram, probably told Charlie Baines I was a smart guy; I'd invent one. But of course I hadn't.

So he broke away, shuffled back to his truck.

"It's okay. He gets moody," Charlie Baines said. "He said you were the kind of person who . . ."

"Maybe we all get moody," I said.

"Someday I'll tell you his secret," Charlie Baines said. "Has he told you mine? Yet?"

"No," I said. "No, he hasn't."

"Well, he will. . . . Soon." Charlie Baines cleared his throat, pinched his mouth. "The world's a whispering place," he said. "I can assure you." And he picked up a stone and threw it . . . farther than I could, with the naked eye, follow. Then he picked up another larger stone and threw that so that it *whonked* off of the Datsun's hood.

I could speak of the unarisen. In my life. And go on. And on. Because I've waited. Clearly. I've postponed. Opportunities— for instance, to plant a field of strawberries or press olive oil. Still submerged. By fear, perhaps—the Boy fearing the Man. Chances, callings—to do more than finish. To . . . Lord knows: Make wine. Build a summer house. Celebrate a child's birth- day. Devise a scheme. Fly-fish. Say good-bye to a father. Ask someone with a religious vision what they've seen. Concoct a huge crock of oyster stew on the Fourth of July just for my neighbors. Erect a monument. Establish a trust. Love a woman. I am perhaps uneasy in regard. Have been. Perhaps . . .

Charlie West drove us back to town, locked, it seemed, in a bank of refusal. We drove against a sky stained with fruits and berries. I tried to listen for whispers and kept imagining tools—every tool I'd as much as set a hand to. Jackhammers; awls. Socket wrenches. Fine battery-operated sanders. Every tool of my life. There was a whole set of pipe fitters and a band saw. Augers, axes, wedges, countersinks. A spirit level and a Craftsman power drill. It was almost night, and it was like a trade show—hardware dealers and home-center retailers, all in my brain, hauling out their wares.

That same night, Lacey Ames and I made love under her pyramid, and directly afterward she began to shake and moan all about her dead sister. She was only half a person, she said. She was only half of what had been meant to be in the world! She said the doctors had all told her mother that her sister, Amber, had, truth told, *drowned* in Lacey. I said, "Lacey, no." I said, "Lacy, please; definitely not; no, people/family don't *drown* in each other. You're not half; you're whole." And then *I* started to cry—because I'd been only half right, partly candid. People *do* drown in each other—and there we were—clinging, rocking; two people set out upon an ocean.

And you could hear the wind. Somewhere. Outside. Lone and singular. Barely alive; barely breathing. And then that one wind you could hear crisscrossing another, rippling over the sea.

In the quiet, then, and trying to make up for holding back, I told Lacey about the treasure. I revealed the ship. It felt so enclosed and private—there inside the Lucite and rosewood of her pyramid, whatever the crosswinds, and she was astonished. In part I'd handed on my amazement. We imagined masts rising up out of the desert crust. "Justin, if I could see that," Lacey Ames said. "If I could be there and see that, I think my twin . . . " She didn't finish her sentence. But then she tried again: "I'd be bigger . . . I'd be more . . . And she'd . . . !"

For a week, every day, Charlie West asked, "Do you have a plan?" And every day, I was forced to admit, "No, I don't." All the outside light would be like some wide, listening ear—to which I'd have to confess that nothing in me useful had arrived.

But then, out of the blue, Christensen Foundries called Charlie Baines and said, "Stop your drilling! Stop your testing! We're letting all our short-term leases expire." It was because they'd found a better venture just this side of the California line. Twenty casinos. Hunting. Fishing. All on Indian Nation. Death Valley Lakes I, II, and III! We'd all be given a gift; all we had to do was wait.

So wait we did. But waiting generates, and every week there'd be that much more corkscrew gold. Blackened tatters of sailcloth. A clot of sedimentary rock; inside, a diamond. Germs from the darkness. Charlie Baines confided, one afternoon, that when he'd been twelve, a gang of boys had set another boy on fire. He said the other boy had been in the hospital for a month for skin grafts. "I don't know why I'm telling this," Charlie Baines said.

Charlie West—out of a strange, eerie warm-up of hummed harmonics—confessed to wanting to be an ice-skater. Between the ages of eight and fifteen, he said, he'd practiced five hours a day on some artificial ice in Oklahoma. He'd tried out for Disney on Ice. He said there was a rink out near the Showboat where he went still and dreamed of triple axels. With almost every song on the radio, he said, he thought, *Is this a song I could skate to?* I asked Charlie Baines, afterwards, was that Charlie West's big secret? Charlie Baines said no . . . no. No. He'd never heard that one before; it was just something that had arisen.

I began, inside then, to search out *my* secret. What I'd never told, am not telling. I'd begun in one place, gone to another, then another. I'd done cabinets. When I was just twelve, my father drove to Alaska to repair the pipeline and fish. My mother went to do promotional work for a Lincoln-Mercury dealership down in Taos, New Mexico. All that's, though, record. What isn't? What haven't I let surface?

I have a wild dream, sometimes, of sea cucumber and coral. I wake up, cupped in some soft and underwater hand. With me, a woman; her skin like the belly of a fish, flesh all in jade and salmon. Shades and rippled. Awake then, we walk—the life of the underwater everywhere, flung like pennants, whole savannahs of seagrass. And I feel—*we* feel, I think—at once close and open. And close and open is what we do. With all that's there. In this place, dream, this wild dream sometimes, somehow, I'm given over to.

One night, there was a message on my machine. It was from a Larry Hart, who was one of Lacey Ames's pit bosses at the Luxor. He wondered might we both find some time? For coffee? Whatever. When I asked Lacey what she imagined he wanted, her breathing skipped, color changed. She said she'd sort of told Larry Hart about the ship.

"Why?" I asked.

"I just—I don't know—got excited," she said. "He'd been talking about all these things: how he'd always been hoping, counting, planning. But lately, he said, there'd been only disappointment. He was saying how pretty much everything was always less. He said you dreamed, then . . . what? What? Nothing happened. Where was the dream? He was saying people use other people. So I said no, no, no. That wasn't it at all. Like, so, for instance . . . And I told the story."

I called Larry Hart, said okay, sure, coffee. He asked could he bring a friend? I asked, A friend? *one*? How many people had he told? He said one; a single person. I said fine; bring him along. That's the thing: you dream, next there are five hundred people.

We met at the New Country on East Desert Inn. Larry Hart's friend's name was Cobb. He was a seismic engineer. They asked to hear Lacey Ames's story from me. I asked Larry Hart could he first say back what *he'd* heard. And certain things he knew; others he didn't. Lacey hadn't told everything. The basic facts, though, he had: a ship . . . buried somewhere under the desert, down a hundred, two hundred feet . . . with the ship, booty. Treasure. Gold.

He asked did we have a claim? How were we going to bring the ship to the surface? The raising, he said, was why he'd brought Cobb along. Cobb, it seemed, had a technique using certain elements of harmonics, others of magnetic resonance. It was a technique used against avalanches and on certain archeological projects. He said it was basically molecular agitation—Cobb had been a fraternity brother—but what, after all was he doing blabbering on; Cobb could explain it, most likely, much better.

And so Cobb tried. And I tried to follow. The basic sense was, everything was reversible. *Concrete* then could reverse and become a colloidal suspension, in turn become just dry mix and clear water. Following that, you could, in theory, go down one and two hundred feet and, with the right resonancing application, right infusion—however many gallons of water, brine—return packed silicate to seabed and float the ship.

"He's done amazing things in the Gobi," Larry Hart said, "and in the Antarctic. He's made underground cities no one suspected were there just—bingo!—*appear*."

Obviously, Larry Hart wanted in.

I told Larry Hart and Cobb that I was not engaged alone. I had partners. This was a shared enterprise. I would have to inquire.

"I just want to leave you with one question," Larry Hart said. "One question, really, for all of us, anyone anywhere in the universe pursuing this, to think about."

And what was that? I asked. What would that one question be?

"Who owns the Wealth of the Past?" he said.

Who owns the . . . ? Who . . . ? It was a decent question— one I had no real answer to. So I passed it on. "Who owns the Wealth of the Past?" I asked Lacey Ames. She gave up. "Who owns the Wealth of the Past?" I asked both of the Charlies. Charlie West shrugged. Charlie Baines said he'd heard that

there *wasn't* a past anymore; it was all free market and global-
ization; there was just present and future. Charlie Baines also
said that we ought to talk seriously with Cobb and Larry Hart.

I wondered again: *my* secret—might it have gotten lost?
In . . . whatever, *transit*. Relocation. The redistributions, such
as they were, of my growing up? my family. Might my secret
have *been*, once, there in the past, but then the past had dis-
solved itself into tar? Into petrocarbons? Which could be—
yes, certainly, if dug up—*dated* but which, still, had no life?
Not measurably. No real destiny? Was that possible?

We brought Larry Hart and Cobb in, though we agreed neither would get shown the site until (1) all of the Christensen
short-term leases expired and (2) our own personal lease was
down in black and white as a matter of record. Larry Hart
carried on a bit about that with Lacey Ames: What was our
problem? Didn't we trust him? What did we think he would
do? Lacey Ames said what was he talking about? He was a pit
boss in a casino. What did he expect?

The color of the sun changed: grew more red, less perfect,
more distended. Perhaps, though, it was just the season, the
time of year. And more than a thousand Asians arrived in
town—Filipinos, Koreans, Japanese. Don't ask why; I'm not
sure; I'm just saying.
    Charlie West and I got moved north, outside Indian Springs,
to do work on Northwest Passage Lakes II and III. Lacey Ames
began to see her twin sister, Amber. It would be night; Amber
would appear—inside the pyramid, float at the foot of Lacey's
bed. And they would talk. Lacey Ames seemed very happy.
She said a great wound would fall soon from the earth. She
asked would I be willing—not, of course, forever but for a
while—to be her dead twin sister's lover, love them both, so
that we might all be of a single flesh. "Lie still!" she'd say. I'd

be in her bed—naked on the far side of her pyramid. "Wait for Amber." She'd have dangled crystals that sang, one against the other, like wind chimes and have lit an almond candle, only a pinpoint but bright. "Still! She's coming! We just have to be patient. She'll arrive."

Cobb had a laboratory. Actually, Cobb had a garage strewn with tools, tables, and equipment. He had set up a huge terrarium in which he'd buried a model four-masted ship, which you could see through the terrarium's glass at one side. The ship was black and gold. It had parchment sails and was about eighteen inches in length by six wide. Above were about five feet of sand. Maybe three weeks after he'd been signed on, he invited the two Charlies and myself over. "I want you to see something," he said.

"Should you keep the garage door open?" Charlie Baines said.

"It gets stuffy," Cobb said. "Watch."

Cobb had what looked like X-ray machines, *four* of them, aimed in at the prow, stern, port, and starboard of the ship. He'd buried four what looked like copper plates deep within the sand under the ship at points. Above the terrarium, he'd suspended nearly a dozen tuning forks—from which almost invisible wires traced themselves into and through the sand.

"Ultimately this will be much more sophisticated," Cobb said. "Nevertheless . . ."

"Right—*nevertheless* . . ." Charlie West said.

"Shut up," Charlie Baines said.

Cobb powered the X-rays. We could hear them surge on and whir. Using a metal rod, he began tapping the tuning forks, resonating a more and more intense chord, his face beaming to beat the band. Finally, with a hand-held remote, he shuttered the X-rays so that, all around, they were like a nest of cameras.

"Good...good!" Cobb kept repeating. "Perfect...wonderful!"

Then—all of us there and watching—the whitish sand around the model shivered and quaked, agitated, lost its density and changed color—green first, white-green, then a turquoise. It began to liquefy. Next: two things! The boat floated slightly. The sand dropped and began to form a new white-sand bed *beneath* where the boat was listing. Cobb was giggling now. It was amazing!

I remember once—fifteen—I had a coach and a girlfriend. It was winter, and I'd broken the assist record for my school. Coach kept referring to me as Duke and Blue Devil. My girlfriend, Spring McKenzie, crusaded on weekends in Youth for Christ. She believed a person's skin to be a stained-glass window and had ridden buses to conventions where she'd learned that. Often she came back looking like she'd spent her whole time giving blood. I thought a lot that year about professional basketball and about colored glass and about the circulatory system. Somehow, seeing Cobb's crazy imagination at work reminded me. A person's stories need water and air. Secrets live in igneous rock.

Our air was busier in the city and filled with languages. Something began to scribble the light like a bright hatch of insects—rumor or hush. The air rippled like gelatin all around the deuces-wild video-poker machines. One morning the *Las Vegas Review-Journal* carried the composite drawing of a ship— Viking, it said. Possibly Phoenician. People had reported vessels sailing into their dreams.

And there were men walking in and out of the Forum Shops at Caesars with metal detectors, women in wet suits at the foot of the volcano at the Mirage. One Thursday night, eating shrimp cocktail at the Golden Gate, I caught three people doodling what I swear were schooners on their paper napkins. Something was where it hadn't been—*out*, like a rib sticking out of a person's thigh.

The Christensen leases expired in October and our own leases began. We called ourselves Venture Voyages and engaged in visits to Cobb. He had a new tank—ten feet square—and demonstrated—via different strip-copper perimeters—that he could work his dry-sand-to-sea magic almost anywhere. Liquefied, sand would pillow one, then a larger model boat. All unliquefied sand fell, always, outside the lines, fine as a glazier's dust.

All Charlie Baines needed to do, Cobb explained, was—when the time came—determine how far any of the treasure had spilled. And how deep. Then he would lay the copper and enclose it all—repeating there in the desert all the riddles of his garage. And we would salvage a ship.

Sometimes my head could be an aquarium—filled up with the ruddered tail, the dorsal fins of memories and half-memories: things I knew, things I really didn't. Grandparents. Basketball hoops. There was a gabled house circled with porches and slashed with heat vents. A field of corn. A rolling orchard of peach trees, cherry trees. Old cars. Horses. Outside: a snaking clothesline with a thousand sheets. Sunflowers. Morning glories. A woman—Lacey Ames mostly, but then not. Spring McKenzie. You could see beyond her skin, details, the face of Christ. And there was myself laughing. Then bent in pain. Myself making a perfect pass for a reverse layup. What I dreamed fading away then coming close again—offering, taking what it held away.

We kept Larry Hart guessing for as long as we could before Cobb nodded and we drove them both out to the site. I used blindfolds, which Cobb felt to be fine but which Larry Hart recoiled against. What kind of small-time operators, after all, did we think we were? Charlie West said, "Good; you got it! Nail-on-the-head. It exactly! Small-time operators. Put the blindfolds on."

When we got there, Larry Hart sniffed and scraped and moved his tongue in the air like a coyote. "Creosote," he said. "A lot of creosote." He walked this way . . . that. Checked the core samplings. His hands raked his hair. Cobb troweled soil specimens into different jars. He asked Charlie Baines what his best estimate of *dead center* was, then, when Charlie said, he scooped sand up and ate it. There were lots of birds—late afternoon—mostly throatier birds: rock dove, grouse, road-runners. The air was hot and dry and curried and the color of wheat.

Larry Hart asked, "Do you know what *to prosper* is?" And he delivered a small sermon or a kind of miniature essay on *to prosper*. To prosper, he said, was to know the comforts of sunlight, and to prosper was to be drinking heady liquor on a veranda overlooking the sea. To prosper was to have no need of clothes and to be always within touching distance of a lover. To pros-per was, when you needed to move through air, to move there, and when you needed to move through water to move *there* and, when you needed to move across land, to move *there*: all places simply, easily. To prosper was to have houses appointed for you wherever you went. To prosper was to be known in restaurants. To prosper was to be in the company of others who were, all of them, called prosperous. It was to be amused by your picture in a weekly magazine. It was to build a build-ing that cost more than a million dollars a day simply to main-tain. To prosper was to endow a school of medicine, to own a professional basketball team, to control an airline, build a movie studio. To prosper was to have any of the great art museums in the world ask for *your* collection, please, on loan. To prosper was to never, ever, imagine tomorrow.

Secrecy is like a lover, but the known enemy of that lover is *rumor*. Rumor circles the bed where secrecy dreams. Larry Hart had plans—you could see—and we were not the friends of his plans. Enrapt as we were with the ship-under-the-desert, the sea-in-the-sand, ours was not the same urgency.

To bury a two-mile circle of copper flashing a hundred and ninety feet below the desert floor is no easy task, and it took Cobb the better part of three weeks. He had to carve a circle with an auger, protect it with reinforced concrete conduit. And all the copper had to be woven from filaments so that it would bow easily, snake and corner. Every hour or so, he would have to stop and clean all of his equipment. The desert began to smell at times like sulfuric acid, at other times, like a lake of acetone.

The Forest Service arrived, six men in as many Cherokees. They asked what it was we were doing—what our operation was. Charlie West grinned. He said, "Brain surgery." He produced our leases. Chad, the ranger-in-charge, said, "There are only so many things you can do to the earth." Cobb said he had advanced degrees in geophysics and mineralogy and thought he knew that. The Forest Service drove their Cherokees off, but the next day it was the FBI, twice the number, in Broncos, *white* Broncos, all with radiation counters. What were we doing? they asked. Rumor was we were setting up *fusion procedures,* tapping into the trapped emissions from Nevada's underground testing. They said that any energy in the desert was the federal government's and were we all aware of the penalties for misappropriation of government things? They walked the property off, swaying their counters like vacuum cleaners. Every once in a while, one of the agents would think he had something—but then didn't. After an hour, they drove off. On the flats and against everything that was expanse, they looked like Tonka toys on a dirt patch.

A truck of Guatemalans showed up, Spanish voices in the air like a truck radio as they approached. They said the word was there was work. We said there wasn't. But that didn't stop them. They spilled and piled out of their truck anyway, flooded the space, below encircled with copper—kneeling, taking their shirts off, washing themselves with the coarse sand—chests, under their arms, faces, hair—as if it all, the sand, were some estuary—before they remounted their flatbed and rolled off. We could see them meeting another truck, stacked as well with bodies, perhaps a mile away. We could see them stop, see the two trucks, talking to one another. Then both trucks drove off.

So, although certainly we'd contained the secret, rumor spread—not unlike an oil spill. Boats were sailing into the dreams of everybody, clogging the harbors of the bipolar. Entire branches of government exercised themselves about resource depletions, losses of energy. Early one morning, Charlie Baines said, Tony and Roger Christensen drove their Lexus in. "What is it you haven't told us?" they asked. "I did my job for you," Charlie Baines told them. "I reported everything you asked."

"What about what we *didn't*? what we *didn't* ask for?" both the Christensens wanted to know.

Sometimes Lacey Ames was Lacey; sometimes she was the departed spirit of her twin sister, Amber. Lacey said that how I could tell was Amber's body had its own light and was hard as bone in some places, soft as musk oil in others. "If I come apart in your hands but then am, like, tight as reflex against your belly, then I'm Amber." And, somehow, I began to believe in her being almost as much as Lacey—especially with the bed dark and the pyramid glinting with citronella.

We couldn't stem the flood. As if drawn to a shore, people came, rigged up with sonar instruments, nets, camcorders, sonographs.

"Hey, look," Charlie Baines might try, "sorry to disappoint— but this is just the desert."

Still, men came in white casino stretch limos: Was it true ours was the site of a new two-thousand-room mega-brothel? There were entire families with cherry pickers, brimming minibuses of Japanese willing to commit their lifetimes, tanned young women in hard hats saying no problem; they'd done Saudi Arabia and knew offshore rigs.

Always, though, Charlie Baines was appropriate. He was gentle. He turned everyone away, back toward whatever their origin. Whatever secret it was that had shimmed the air around them.

So then: what was *my* secret? *Was* there one? I know I made promises to Spring McKenzie that I never kept and never thought of keeping and never meant. I know I walked off from a basketball scholarship to St. John's University, the day my father said, over the phone all the way from Anchorage, "You're too small." I know I started a grassfire once—burned half a peach orchard. I don't know. Do those qualify? I can't say. I can't say—though certainly all are moments when I held my heart in my hand, felt the truth of it in the music it made and didn't make but then pretended it wasn't my heart, that it was something else—a jawbreaker, a socket wrench.

I had trouble sleeping. I was restless with Lacey, or perhaps restless with Amber. When Lacey said she was Amber, she'd leave streaks of blood on me and a kind of slick, like glue, like the crushed needles of an Engelmann spruce; they gave off that smell. And Lacey would always want to take me to the shower and soap me afterward. "Amber's frightened," she'd say. "Amber's scared and she has reason."

Finally though—all preparations done, hope stretched beyond tensile strength—we set True Salvage for a predawn, mid-week and on a Thursday. Any of Cobb's apparatus—pumps, generators, maybe a dozen Dolby Sound amplifiers—sat covered with tarpaulins in a truck. It was Wednesday. There'd been thunderheads Tuesday night, but they'd gone. Cobb had laid all his wiring out and given us jobs. We rehearsed. Time, to Cobb, was critical. This was not a diversion—in no way, in *no way* was it a diversion—it was procedure.

Larry Hart had bought a dozen new suits and he looked strange, fancied out as he was, in silk and poplin against the rabbitbrush, like the wrong idea for a layout in *GQ* magazine. "Pay attention," Cobb appealed. And we did. We got all the connections, the setups, down to less than forty minutes.

Lacey Ames dealt Wednesday night. And for a while I went over to the Luxor so as to be near. I played some dice. I would see them roll and turn up—a four/three, a six/two—but then the stickman would announce a nine, and when I looked, sure enough, it would be a nine—a three/six. I played cards, swore I'd been dealt a queen/eight, looked again to see and it was an ace/four. So I stopped gambling.

I went down to visit King Tut's Tomb, but it was closed for repairs, so I went, instead, into the coffee shop and ordered *huevos rancheros,* trying to imagine the morning.

Lacey Ames's shift let her go about two, and we drifted across the street to the Tropicana for a cappuccino, where Lacey Ames started to cry. She said she didn't really know why she was crying, except her whole head had been full to bursting with Iowa recently. I asked why Iowa, and she said, "I don't know; I have no idea; at first I thought it was just Illinois." Then what *I* said was—and it came out of the blue—"Lacey: I want to make a promise to you. Except, I'm sorry, I don't know yet—what that promise is."

We drove out. To the site. The air was warm. Unnaturally. You could smell yucca and giant Joshua. Lacey Ames said she heard owls. "I'm really worried about Amber," she said. And I said, "I know," though the words "I know" were like light taking up space in water.

Everybody was there. Both Charlies. Larry Hart—dressed in a linen suit and panama hat. Of course, Cobb. There were halogen floodlamps set up. Charlie Baines had a tureen of Texas chili, and there were pots of coffee on his Coleman stove. "Why not start?" Larry Hart said.

Cobb only shook his head. "Everything," he said, "in time. In its place. This is an operation."

The time set was 4:27 A.M. And when it arrived, we all cracked into moving. Charlie West strode from generator to generator. He unrolled electrical cables from their spools. Certain coils had been buried around the circle, with Ziploc bags fastened around their three-pronged plugs, and I checked those out, blew away any sand, hooked them up. Larry Hart and Charlie Baines rolled the huge X-ray machines out, so that they sat at the four points of the compass and around the circle. Cobb checked that the machines were aligned—directed them at the copper flashing.

Lacey Ames read down the checklist every four minutes or so; her job: keep us organized and on schedule. We unloaded pumps and placed them. We did the same with amplifiers and resonators. It took both Charlies, Larry Hart, and myself for the unloading. Cobb had built special-alloy ramps. There was a pulley system on the truck. We had a huge refrigerator dolly. Thirty-eight minutes after we had started, we were done. We were ready. My heart was hammering.

"Exactly five-oh-five," Lacey Ames reported.

"Five minutes . . . we start," Cobb said. "So why don't we double-check all of the connections?"

Which we did.

We were ready.

At 5:10, Cobb began. He began throwing switches and, with a remote, setting off X-ray machines. "Stand back . . . stand back," Cobb kept saying. "You don't want to be too close."

I kept seeing Cobb's home terrarium and multiplying it. But the world is, finally, so much more than a garage.

"OhmyGod!" Larry Hart began. "OhmyGod. . . . OhmyGod, I can actually *feel* it!"

Which was true. We could. Feel it actually. Way beneath and all around: the place changing. The desert, starting to fold and roil, like a nest of snakes, activating, starting its memory—a thousand, two thousand, three thousand years ago: a millennium. *Once!* you could almost hear the desert thinking. *Once!*

And then, the whole coarseness of what Cobb had encircled with his copper, we could see, softening. Earth!—the raw cereal of its sere compounding we could see slake away, blanch, whiten. There was the hint of sky now—*in* it, *through* it— that faint cerulean, that blue, the tint of life, supported life, reflection. It was beginning to decide: *If once . . . then . . . why not Again? Why not Ocean!? Sea!*

Cobb had said the whole transformation would take just a trace under an hour—that at 5:10 the desert would be what we had always known but that at 6:03 an ancient ship would *float* in the same place and that, leagues beneath it, on the ocean bed, there'd be gold.

So then, how do I tell you what it was I felt and that, when felt, I knew it to be of the inside of Lacey's canopy and within her bed? It was all my lungs. It was my bones. It was my breath being in my head and my tears flooding into that—washed by all the people, all the places, that I'd left. It was the sense of something never imagined, a gift, being extended by another, some person you have never known or thought you'd known, yet there she is and in this amazing posture of regard.

At about 5:28 or 5:29, it was Charlie Baines who noticed: a long, what-seemed-like-endless caravan began to wind itself along the rutted trail leading in from the east. Automobiles of every description, flatbeds, pickup trucks, motorcycles with sidecars, Vespas, whole families on foot, people in work clothes with their sleeves rolled up, people in dress uniforms, children and dogs, vendors carrying balloons, groups with instruments. Charlie Baines pointed off and said, "Look!" Larry Hart said, *"Fuck!"*

But they all simply spread out—up and away—and circled. Circled this place to which no person was born. Nobody charged. Nobody intruded. They just all wanted to see and be there when it all happened.

We are all pilgrims, I think, standing on a beach. From nowhere, gulls appeared—ten, a thousand—swung, looped, dove over our secret—cries, hungry and raucous in the Nevada air. It began. Quake; tremble: a cloy of brine, thick and sudden in the dawn. Then booming—sort of. A roar; a chord—seeming like everything below the surface of the earth has been struck together, like timpani.

The ocher ground ripples and turns blue. Cobb's a genius. Masts rise from the belly of the earth's rumble, fill and swell. Decayed rigging; tattered sail! And for an instant—an instant only; short as when numbers on a pair of dice change before your eyes—we are all there in the presence of a grand, a tall-masted ancient ship as it sails upon the high plateau of the Nevada desert!

And then . . . and then . . .

Then the ship decomposes, dissolves. To ash; to dust; to filament, atomizing matter in the new-lit and copper-colored sky. And Lacey Ames screams, shrieks out, "Amber!" "One thing I failed to think about," Cobb will later confess. "One thing . . . is the effect of a very different and more-oxidizing air on a vessel submerged so deep . . . and for so long."

Still—it was not phantom—we all saw it. And each could as easily turn to the other, standing left or right, and remark together. Witness; confirm. Secure that such a thing had happened and make it a memory.

Oh, and yes: The treasure? The trove? If not the ship itself? I suppose, a happier ending.

Keeping Cobb's apparatus manned, we all entered, naked to our ankles, strapped air tanks on our backs, and, one by one, broke the surface of the ancient sea.

And, yes, our treasure was there: spread on the deepest sand, just as Cobb had engineered and predicted. And we collected it—baskets, nets—helped each other. Brought it up. And, in that, all were made rich—though none beyond our wildest dreams. Because wildest dreams, I see now, trace a different destiny. They assume the air. They linger. They hold a momentary discourse. Then retrace their steps . . . into wherever—whatever fathomless sea it is that wildest dreams arise in, sail from.

Western Literature Series

■ ■ ■

The Track of the Cat
Walter Van Tilburg Clark

Shoshone Mike
Frank Bergon

Condor Dreams and Other Fictions
Gerald W. Haslam

A Lean Year and Other Stories
Robert Laxalt

Cruising State:
Growing Up in Southern California
Christopher Buckley

The Big Silence
Bernard Schopen

Kinsella's Man
Richard Stookey

The Desert Look
Bernard Schopen

Winterchill
Ernest J. Finney

Wild Game
Frank Bergon

Lucky 13:
Short Plays About Arizona, Nevada, and Utah
edited by Red Shuttleworth

The Measurable World
Katharine Coles

Keno Runner
David Kranes

TumbleWords: Writers Reading the West
edited by William L. Fox

From the Still Empty Grave: Collected Poems
A. Wilber Stevens

Strange Attraction:
The Best of Ten Years of ZYZZYVA
edited by Howard Junker

Wild Indians & Other Creatures
Adrian C. Louis

Bad Boys and Black Sheep: Fateful Tales from the West
Robert Franklin Gish

Stegner: Conversations on History and Literature
Wallace Stegner and Richard W. Etulain

Warlock
Oakley Hall

The Iris Deception
Bernard Schopen

Low Tide in the Desert: Nevada Stories
David Kranes